TOMMY
and the
SLOTH

Allan Frewin Jones

Illustrated by Paul Cox

SIMON & SCHUSTER
YOUNG BOOKS

Text copyright © Allan Frewin Jones 1992
Illustrations copyright © Paul Cox 1992

First published in Great Britain in 1992
by Simon & Schuster Young Books

Photoset in North Wales by
Derek Doyle & Associates, Mold, Clwyd.
Printed and bound in Great Britain by
the Guernsey Press Co Ltd,
Guernsey, the Channel Islands

Simon & Schuster Young Books
Campus 400
Maylands Avenue
Hemel Hempstead HP2 7EZ

British Library Cataloguing in Publication Data available

ISBN 0 7500 0922 5
ISBN 0 7500 0923 3 (pb)

Chapter One

"I see Great Aunt Tomasina is off on her travels again."

Tommy peered round the edge of her mother's newspaper. Headlines and blurred colour photos lolloped around the page, spaced out by neat little stacks of type. Looking oddly out of place was a small square black and white photograph of Great Aunt Tomasina in a pith helmet. Circa 1933.

"Where to this time?" asked Tommy's father. He was reading the *Highway Code*. He was going to pass his driving test this time. Third time lucky.

"Bhajangaya," read Tommy's mother.

"Where on earth's that?"

"Nepal. Up the top of India. You know."

Tommy looked longingly at the fuzzy photo of her great aunt.

Tomasina DeCourcey Octavia Murgatroyd was the only really interesting relative Tommy had. The only relative on her mother's side. All the other uncles and aunts and cousins came by the handful like sweets out of a jar. But Great Aunt Tomasina was one in a million. She was fantastically old and fantastically eccentric. She lived in a large peculiar house in the elderly, southern part of town. It had once been posh, but the posh people had all gone somewhere else and the area had become a bit creaky and wheezy. She lived in what was called Genteel Poverty. Every now and then she would go exploring to drum up enough money to keep a roof over her head.

She had a very particular attitude to exploring. If, while hacking her way through a South American rain forest, she happened upon a tribe of completely unknown people, minding their own business and living their lives the way they wanted to, she would quietly tiptoe in the opposite direction and not tell anyone.

Any normal explorer, as Tommy's father had often observed, any *normal* explorer would rush off to Civilisation and then gallop back to the tribe as quickly as possible with film crews and notepads and squadrons of scientists and anthropologists prodding and poking about so that the tribe could be properly studied. Learned papers would be written, lecture tours would be undertaken and a best-selling book would be written. Not to mention a TV series. And chat shows. That, pointed out Tommy's father, is how explorers get rich and famous.

"But she *is* famous," said Tommy.

"But not rich," said her father. "And that's the point."

Tommy's mother murmured something about exploitation and turned the page.

Her father said: " 'If anything falls from your vehicle, stop as soon as you can with safety and remove it from the carriageway.' " Deathless wisdom from the *Highway Code*.

Tommy looked at the clock, climbed into her shoulder bag and set off down the little row of terraced houses that led to the railway bridge and across the road to school.

She thought wistfully of Great Aunt Tomasina and her glamorous travels. Tommy felt a special affinity with her great aunt. After all, she had been named after her. Not everyone these days gets called Tomasina. Not that she *was* called Tomasina very often – Tommy, if she was lucky and Tom-tom if she wasn't. She only got called Tomasina when she'd done something wrong. "Tomasina Petheridge, this exercise book is a disgrace. You know very well the rules about drawing on the outer cover." That sort of thing.

They visited Great Aunt Tomasina in her extraordinary house three times a year. Once on or near Great Aunt Tomasina's birthday, to give presents; once on or near Tommy's birthday, to receive presents; and once on or near Christmas Day, to swap presents. Tommy never understood why it was apparently impossible to visit Great Aunt Tomasina without all this present business. But apparently it wasn't, and that was that.

The best part of these visits was when Great Aunt Tomasina would lean back in her huge old wing-backed armchair with her feet stretched towards a roaring real wood fire and tell stories about her adventures.

It was at these times that Tommy had learned that Great Aunt Tomasina had scaled Everest seven months and ten days before Sir Edmund Hillary and Sherpa Tensing. During these tales Tommy's father would gaze out of the window and try to think of reasons why they had to leave early; and her mother would smile in a mysterious way and not say anything.

"You will notice, my dear," Great Aunt Tomasina would say, "that when people speak of the first conquest of Everest, they always refer to Sir Edmund Hillary as the first *man* to have reached the uttermost peak. The first *man*, my dear." And Great Aunt Tomasina would sniff. "At least let us grant them the grace of being embarrassed enough not to declare Sir Edmund the first *person* to climb Everest." And then Great Aunt Tomasina would lean forward and tap Tommy's knee with a knotty finger.

"Always watch out for that, my dear. Always watch out for them when they speak of the first *man* to do anything. That usually means there was a woman there first that they're trying to hush up."

And Tommy would gaze at her with eyes like full moons and mull over a few ideas in her mind ... Francis Chichester: the first *man* to sail single-handed round the world; Yuri Gagarin: the first *man* in space; Roger Bannister: the first *man* to run a mile in under four minutes ... and wonder if Great Aunt Tomasina had got there first, and that it had all been kept quiet for some reason.

Under Great Aunt Tomasina's spell in her extraordinary old house, everything seemed possible. It wasn't until Tommy was in the car being driven home by her mother and heard her father remark: "She lives in a world of her own, that woman," that the bubble of belief would burst and she'd begin to wonder if Great Aunt Tomasina's tales could *really* be true.

A few weeks went by. Tommy's father failed his third driving test and had to be comforted by her mother and tiptoed around by Tommy for three or four days.

It was curious. When Tommy failed things at school she got told off or at least frowned at. When her father failed his driving test he was cossetted and crooned over. Tommy felt sure Great Aunt Tomasina's endless store of wisdom would hold the key to that sort of puzzle; but Great Aunt Tomasina was off adventuring somewhere and hadn't been heard of since April the seventeenth when she had sent a postcard to Tommy from Muscat telling her she was waiting for a dhow to take her across the Arabian Sea.

It was the middle of May, on a bleak and rainy day that was doing its best to act the part of early February, when the news broke that the boat in which Great Aunt Tomasina had been traversing the Arabian Sea had been washed up wrecked in the Gulf of Kutch.

There had been no survivors. The authorities said that the dhow could have been wrecked at any time in the previous month, and that there was no hope of anyone being found alive. The news was in all the papers. Tommy cried a great deal and actually screamed when her father bought her some roller skates to take her mind off it.

"I don't *want* my mind taken off it!" she yelled through the keyhole of her locked bedroom door. "And I don't want any roller skates."

"Leave her be," said her mother. "She's better left alone. Remember the trouble we had after the gerbil."

At the table Tommy's father would shake his head and talk about the tragedy of it all. The tragedy being, in his mind, that a lady of Great Aunt Tomasina's advanced years should be sufficiently unhinged as to attempt to cross the Arabian Sea in a dhow in the first place. After all, there were such things as aeroplanes.

Tommy's mother said very little about it, but collected the obituaries from all the newspapers and glued them with loving care into a scrap book bought especially for that purpose from the local branch of W.H. Smith.

Tommy's father said this was ghoulish and morbid.

Tommy's mother said she didn't care and could he please address his attention to the *Highway Code* and not bother making assinine comments on things about which he knew nothing. Tommy's mother was not looking forward to having to soothe him after a fourth failed driving test.

Tommy's grief quietened down without losing its grip on her heart. She stopped crying, but was no less aware of a great sense of loss. Sometimes she would sit on her bed with her mother's Great Aunt Tomasina Obituary Scrap Book open in her lap and read and re-read the printed facts of Great Aunt Tomasina's amazing life.

She noticed they still refused to make it public that Great Aunt Tomasina had been the first person up Everest.

A long, brown, official-looking envelope arrived, addressed to T. Petheridge. As Tommy's mother's first name was Veronica and her father's first name was David, it should have seemed obvious who the letter was intended for.

"It must be a mistake," said her father. "Since when does Tommy receive letters in manilla envelopes?"

The letter sat unopened on the breakfast table.

Tommy came through and sat down. Her mother pushed the envelope towards her. Tommy sat staring at it for a few moments.

"It's addressed to you," said her mother.

"Are you sure?" said Tommy, who was not used to getting letters of any sort, never mind official ones.

"I'll open it if you like," said her father. "It's bound to be a mistake. A typing error or something."

Her mother slapped her father's encroaching fingers with the butterknife. "It's for Tommy," she said.

Her father grunted and set about his boiled egg in such a manner as to make it plain that he couldn't care less either way.

Tommy carefully peeled open the envelope and slid the letter out.

Ms Tomasina Petheridge,
52 Apeney Towers,
Brick Street,
Louton.

Mssrs Stingemore and Beck, Solicitors,
182 Sleeky Street,
Upper Louton.

Dear Ms Petheridge,

re: *Ms. Tomasina deCourcey Octavia Murgatroyd*
You are invited to the reading of the last will and testament
of the above named, to take place at our offices at 10am on
Friday 12th June. We are pleased to inform you that you
are named as a beneficiary of the Estate of the above.
Trusting you will be able to attend, we are
Yours sincerely,
Edward Stingemore
pp. Stingemore and Beck Solicitors Ltd.

P.S. May we take this opportunity to extend our deepest
sympathies in your great loss.

After she had read it through three or four times Tommy
handed the letter round the table.

"Well," said her father, who got the letter last. "Well."
He seemed to feel the need to say *something*, but clearly
couldn't dredge up anything worthwhile to say.

"That's exciting," said Tommy's mother.

Tommy looked at her. "Is it? I mean ... yes. Yes, I
suppose it is, isn't it?" She sipped her tea. "What does it
mean though, exactly?"

"Exactly what it says," said her father. "Your great aunt has left you something in her will."

Being able to read, Tommy had already cottoned on to this.

"Yes, but left me what?"

"That's what's exciting," said her mother. "It could be anything."

"People sometimes get left enormous amounts of money," said her father.

Tommy's eyes widened. "Do you think so?"

"David, don't be such a goon. You know she didn't have any money."

"You never know. She might have been a miser and we never knew anything about it. She might have cellars in that old house crammed solid with jewels and bank notes."

Tommy's eyes got wider and wider.

"Take no notice," Tommy's mother told her. "Your father's having one of his funny turns." She aimed a deadly look at him. "It's much more likely to be something she's brought back from one of her travels. Something that she was especially fond of and that she particularly wanted you to have. It won't," she glared at her husband, "it *definitely* won't be cellars full of jewels and bank notes."

Great Aunt Tomasina's house was a cornucopia of strange artefacts, gleaned from all over the world. Tommy had spent many hours playing with the more robust of them or gazing at the fragile ones while her great aunt told her their history and how she came upon them.

It might be that fascinating clock from Switzerland with all the doors and secret places that opened up on the hour so that armies of carved mice ran round and round and up and over and in and out while the chimes rang. Or it might be that gloriously ugly statue from India with an elephant's head that squatted in the corner and seemed to know everything. Or the totem pole that was too big to get into any of the rooms and stood, strange and compelling, on the landing with its carved eagle head up the stairwell. Or those tiny white carvings from China that lived in a secret world of their own behind glass in the cabinet by the fireplace. Or ... or ... or ...

Tommy's father heaved a sigh. "That's more likely," he said. "It'll be something big and hideous and completely useless, I expect. Something that'll take a pantechnicon to get home and that'll clutter the house up and collect dust. That's just the sort of trick that woman would play on me."

In the event he was both wrong and right at the same time – but in a way that none of them could have dreamed of.

Chapter Two

The office of Stingemore and Beck, Solicitors, lay up in the rafters of a tall, narrow slice of a long terrace in a side street. They planned to get there in plenty of time, and might have done so if Tommy's father hadn't insisted on navigating. As it was, they arrived at the front door with two minutes to spare.

Tommy was in her best dress. She felt important and slightly overawed. Only the thought that it was Great Aunt Tomasina who had posthumously summoned her to this dark snakey-staired place, stopping her from turning tail and hiding in the car.

They were shown through a series of small rooms that opened into one another. Tommy was surprised at how dingy and tatty it all looked, with moth-eaten people working at moth-eaten desks. The final door lead them to a plushly decorated room full of armchairs and bookcases and a large mahogany desk, behind which Mr Stingemore sat in plump splendour.

Tommy disliked him at first sight. He had one of those chins out of which the bristles grew so fast that he always looked in need of a wash. He had oily black hair scraped thin as watery margarine over his greenish scalp. He had thick drooping lips like a big old fish. And he had gappy yellow teeth. All in all he would have had to have had a supremely pleasant personality to overcome his appearance.

He oozed clammily round the desk and shook Tommy's hand. It was like having someone press a sockful of tapioca into her palm.

"We are very pleased you could come," he said.

Tommy became aware that there were three other people in the room.

"Allow me," said Mr Stingemore, "to introduce you to the other beneficiaries of your great aunt's will."

Tommy was confronted by a stiff white skeleton of a woman. She had straight colourless hair, a straight narrow nose and a lipless mouth. Cold, pale eyes watched from behind winged glasses. Tommy saw straight away that she was a very *watching* sort of person.

"Miss Unity Hitch." The woman extended a bunch of bones in Tommy's direction.

Tommy shook them. The woman smiled. Sort of. The corners of her mouth twitched upwards anyway. She didn't say anything. but Tommy said, "Pleased to meet you," because she was aware of her parents behind her and knew she would be expected to make a good impression.

"Miss Hitch has been your great aunt's nurse for the last few months," said Mr Stingemore.

Tommy didn't know Great Aunt Tomasina had taken on a nurse. She wouldn't have thought she would have needed to be *nursed*. She hadn't known there had been anything wrong with her.

The other two people were men. One was tall and grey haired and immaculately dressed, like something out of a very high-class shop window. He looked as if half a dozen people had spent all day scrubbing and ironing and polishing him. His teeth shone and his fingernails were the cleanest and most carefully manicured Tommy had ever seen.

"Allow me to introduce myself," he said in a voice like honey. "Septimus Murgatroyd, your great aunt's step-brother.'

"Pleez to mee chew," said Tommy in surprise. She'd never heard of him.

"Mr Murgatroyd lives in retirement in the south of France," said Mr Stingemore. "He has come over especially for the reading of the will."

"And let me introduce my companion," said Mr Murgatroyd. "My very great friend, the estimable Mr Alphonso Twigg." Mr Murgatroyd smiled silkily. "A man of considerable talents."

Alphonso Twigg was small and miserable looking, squatting in a suit three times too big for him. He didn't look in the least bit talented. He had the look of someone to whom unfortunate things were always happening. There was an egg stain on his lapel and a piece of sticking plaster on his chin, and he had one of his socks on inside out. He blinked from behind little round glasses.

"Delighted, I'm sure," he said in a dull, sad, nasal voice. He certainly didn't *sound* delighted. He sounded thoroughly dejected.

Tommy's parents shook hands with the three and everyone sat down.

Mr Stingemore took out a lime green folder and laid it on his desk. He droned on for a while about the solemnity and whatever of the occasion. Tommy sneaked glances at the three strangers. She decided Miss Hitch was like frozen vinegar, Mr Murgatroyd like a spoonful of syrup and poor Mr Twigg like one of those sad little sausage rolls that are always left at the end of parties.

These thoughts occupied her until Mr Stingemore came to the interesting bit of the will.

"And now," said Mr Stingemore, "to the part you have been waiting for." He coughed. " To Miss Unity Hitch I leave one hundred pounds and whatsoever of the contents of my wardrobe she feels she would enjoy.' " Miss Hitch's cheeks sank but she said nothing. Tommy felt she wasn't very pleased. " 'To my step-brother Septimus I leave the contents of my jewellery box, in the hope that he will appreciate the value of this gift and not simply the price, and that he will cherish them as family heirlooms.' "

For a second Mr Murgatroyd's face looked ferocious, as if he'd like to jump up and bite Mr Stingemore. His hands wrestled for a moment in his lap then became still. Perhaps only Tommy noticed this, as everyone else was looking at Mr Stingemore. It made her nervous. The little man at his side slumped so that his chin vanished into his collar.

" 'To my beloved great niece, Tomasina Petheridge, I leave my entire estate, omitting only those things already mentioned. My estate consisting of my house and its contents, asking only in return that she shall not sell the house or any of my collection, and that she live there …' "

Tommy heard her father's mouth fall open. There was a second of stunned silence then everyone started talking at once. Everyone except Tommy, who was too happy to speak.

Mr Stingemore tapped a pen on his desk. "If I may finish," he said. " 'There is one further condition. It is that Tomasina Petheridge shall agree to look after and house Noel until such time as he reaches the natural end of his life. After which she may do with the house as she wishes and use my collection in whatever way she sees fit.' " Mr Stingemore closed the lime green folder and leaned back. "That is all," he said.

*

"Unbelievable," said Tommy's father for the umpteenth time. "Absolutely unbelievable."

They were driving home. The meeting had broken up sourly. Miss Hitch had departed with a tart "Good-day." Mr Murgatroyd and his companion had insisted on reading the will themselves, as if they hoped that Mr Stingemore had skipped a line somewhere and got something wrong. Tommy had noticed that Mr Murgatroyd's long, elegant hand had been biting savagely into Mr Twigg's shoulder and that the glum little man had been silently wincing with pain.

Apparently Mr Stingemore had made no error in his reading. Mr Murgatroyd had shaken hands all round, leaving Tommy until last.

"Now then, my dear," he had said suavely, gripping Tommy's fingers. "I wish you well of your inheritance. I certainly do. Very well. Without a doubt. I am sure you deserve every bit of it." And they had left.

"Who's Noel?" Tommy had asked.

"Some pet, I gather," Mr Stingemore had said.

This had surprised Tommy. She'd known nothing of any pet. In fact Great Aunt Tomasina had always had very strong opinions about the keeping or caging of animals. Strong enough for her to have written many long and astringent letters to the newspapers about zoos and such like. Besides which, if Great Aunt Tomasina had a pet, Tommy would have thought they'd have seen it during one of their visits – unless it was a very *new* pet.

It didn't seem like Great Aunt Tomasina at all.

From the back of the car Tommy asked again, "What sort of pet do you think this Noel could be?"

"A dog or a cat," suggested her mother.

"That means at most about fifteen years before we can sell the place," said her father. Her mother looked at him. "I hope it's not a tortoise or a parrot or something like that," he said. "Those things can live for donkey's years."

"I hope it's a cat," said Tommy. "I've always wanted a cat."

"We'll see," said her mother.

The next few weeks were extraordinary. Because Tommy was too young to sign legal documents, all the sheafs of paper that flew about were in her parents' names. Or, to be exact, mostly in her mother's name. Her father bore this with sulky dignity, the sulkiness being very obvious, the dignity less so.

They contacted estate agents and their building society about selling their house. Fortunately Great Aunt Tomasina's house was only a train journey away from Tommy's school. It was a bus, a train and another bus away for her father, as he continuously pointed out. As her mother drove to work, it didn't make much difference to her.

A medium-sized van came and took all their personal belongings. They sold the furniture. There was plenty of furniture in Great Aunt Tomasina's house. Too much, Tommy's father said. Miles too much.

The time whistled by and suddenly they were in Great Aunt Tomasina's hallway with their cases, boxes and carrier bags around their feet. Mr Stingemore solemnly handed the keys over to Tommy, got her mother to sign a last document, then left.

They were standing there wondering what to do next when a thin figure appeared in the open front doorway. It was Miss Hitch. Cold and polite and as bitter as nettles.

Tommy would have liked to be friendly with Miss Hitch, but it was hardly possible. Like making friends with an icicle.

"Have you seen Noel yet?" she asked, after exchanging chilly pleasantries.

They told her they hadn't.

Stiffly Miss Hitch lead them down the hall and sideways under the stairs. They had never really explored the house. They were surprised at how many secret rooms there were. Unexpected doorways and little stairways and dog-legged corridors. They came to a room at the end of a long hall. Tommy began to wonder exactly what sort of creature Noel could be.

On the door someone had painted: QUIET PLEASE. DO NOT DISTURB.

Miss Hitch opened the door. It wasn't an ordinary room. It was all glass and metal, like a greenhouse joined on to the back of the building. It had a door out into the garden – a door with a huge iron bolt on it. The room was stiflingly hot. Through the glass walls they could see the garden. It was a very natural, wild sort of garden. A very exciting, inviting sort of garden without lawns or flower beds or rockeries or plastic ornaments. Just a lively tumble of greenery with flowers and bushes and trees popping up in unusual places.

The room itself was strewn with straw and from the ceiling hung huge tree boughs suspended on chains.

Tommy and her parents looked around for Noel. Her father had a sinking feeling that it might be a monkey: a chimpanzee or a gibbon or the like.

Miss Hitch pointed. From a bough in one corner of the room hung a bundle of fur – greeny-brown.

"That is Noel," she said. Tommy noticed a glint of cruel pleasure in her eye.

Tommy walked into the room. The straw rustled under her feet. She stopped under the still bundle.

"What is it?" she whispered.

"A three-toed South American sloth," said Miss Hitch. "I wish you joy of it."

Chapter Three

A space had to be cleared for the television and record player. This involved a certain amount of rearrangement of the lounge. Things which had sat happily in a nest of dust for who knows how many years found themselves jammed in odd corners or even wrapped in newspaper and put away in cardboard boxes.

The fireplace had always been the centre of the room, but now the armchairs and couch were moved to face the new television set. A large potted fern was taken out into the garden and replaced by the hi-fi. Tommy's father spent half a day arranging the speakers to get the sound balance right.

The lounge was a long room with a bay window at one end and french windows leading on to the garden at the other. Halfway along the room was a square arch with heavy folding doors so that the two halves of the room could be shut off from one another. But the doors were immobile with paint and obviously hadn't been used for years. Tommy was glad of that. She liked the size of the two rooms when they behaved like one room. She wondered which room had spilled into which and how long ago.

There were two fireplaces but only one worked. The other had a tall enamel jug in it, out of which cascaded a spray of dried flowers. The only one Tommy recognised was called honesty. It had seed pods like translucent white coins. There was an upright piano in the back half of the room, but it was locked and no key was obvious. Tommy opened the lid of the piano stool and found sheets and books of music.

"I want to learn to play the piano," she told her parents.

"Hmm," said her father.

"We'll see," said her mother.

"I mean it," said Tommy. "I'm not just *saying* it!"

"It's probably miles out of tune," said her father. "It probably hasn't been played for donkey's years."

"We'll have to find the key," said her mother. "It's a bit pointless talking about it if we can't get the thing open."

"Can I search?" asked Tommy. "Please?"

"Will you be careful?" asked her mother. "I remember that time we got you to help me search for that earring and the house looked like a bomb had hit it."

"Of course I'll be careful," said Tommy. "After all, this does all belong to *me*, doesn't it?"

"Her father looked round at her.

"Well, doesn't it?" she said.

"Sort of," said her father.

"What does sort of mean?"

"It means that legally we're responsible for you until you're eighteen, which means anything that belongs to you is our responsibility as well."

"Do you mean it isn't mine, even though it was left to me? Me particularly?"

"It means," said her mother, "that we'll be ... sort of ... caretakers for you until you're old enough to look after it properly yourself. Like when you go swimming and I look after your clothes and your bag. They're still *your* things,

24

but until you come back I have to look after them for you."

Then her father started explaining the same thing in a much more complicated way. He got quite huffy when both Tommy and her mother wandered off before he'd finished.

Tommy searched for the piano key. She discovered things that it would take pages and pages to list. The house was like a museum, only far more interesting, because she knew that everything had belonged to Great Aunt Tomasina.

She didn't find the key, but she did find an old photo album full of curiously dressed people from years ago.

One picture in particular fascinated her. It was of a small girl in stiff frilly clothes sitting bolt upright in a chair. The girl's hair was in tight ringlets but her face was exactly the same as Tommy's. Under the photograph, in beautiful golden writing, it said: Tommy, aged 10.

The girl's dark eyes gazed down the years at her. Tommy, aged 10.

She showed it to her mother.

"Your great aunt," she said.

"You mean *she* was called Tommy as well?"

"Looks like it."

"Waah!"

Her mother laughed. Waah! was a word Tommy used when ordinary words wouldn't do. Her special word that was for things that thrilled her through and through. Things that were bigger than a dictionary.

Tommy. Great Aunt Tomasina had been called *Tommy* when she was a girl.

Tommy took the photo album to bed.

Her bedroom overlooked the garden. Directly beneath her window the glass roof of Noel's room glowed faintly in the moonlight. She strained to hear any sound of him moving about, but the greenhouse was quite silent and still.

Very late that night, it must have been one or two in the morning, Tommy woke up imagining that she could hear a

25

violin. She lay in the darkness, listening. The sound was very faint, but even when she'd shaken the sleep out of her head she could still hear it.

She crept to her bedroom door and opened it a crack. The rest of the house was dark and the sound did not seem to be coming from downstairs. Not that either of her parents could play the violin, or had any records that she knew of with violins on them.

She turned on her bedside light and pulled a corner of her curtain open. The music stopped immediately. She looked out into the night for a few moments then crept back to bed.

The next morning she had forgotten all about it.

After her father had finished panicking about Noel, Miss Hitch had handed over a small notebook. In large round writing it explained how Noel was to be looked after. Great Aunt Tomasina had opened a special bank account. Noel's needs were to be paid for out of this account. Noel's needs didn't seem very extravagant. A man would come on Saturdays and change the straw that blanketed the floor. The same man would also come on Tuesdays and Thursdays with bundles of leafy branches which he would attach with wire to the boughs that hung in Noel's room. All this was paid for out of Noel's private bank account.

Tommy could tell that Noel's presence in the house bothered her father. She could see it quite clearly. He would be sitting contentedly watching television or mugging up on the *Highway Code* or eating a sandwich and suddenly the creases on his forehead would deepen and she'd know he'd just remembered that in the back of the house, in a glass room full of leaves and heat and straw, Noel hung, being a three-toed South American sloth, and making his life uncomfortable. Noel was an itch that her father couldn't scratch.

Her mother, on the other hand, had started off by trying to make Noel part of the family. She would go into his room every few minutes and coo at him as if he were a baby. As if he were a little child she wanted to make friends with.

"You are a funny looking thing," she'd say to the immobile hammock of greeny-brown fur. "Aren't you? Aren't you a funny looking old thing? Aren't you bored? I bet you're bored, aren't you? I bet you are. I bet you wish you could come in and be with us instead of being stuck out there all on your own. Poor old thing. Poor, funny looking old thing." And she'd reach up to stroke Noel's long straggly fur. "You need a good brush-out, you do."

Tommy borrowed a book from the library. She spent a long time looking for a book specifically about sloths. She didn't find one. There were plenty of thin guides to keeping mice and hamsters and guinea pigs and rabbits and cats and dogs and fish (freshwater and tropical) and even ponies, but nothing as sensible as *A Young Person's Guide to Sloth-Keeping*.

In the end she had to make do with a general animal book which had half a page on sloths and a coloured picture of one. What she didn't need was a photograph of a sloth. What she could have done with was more information about what they did.

On her own one afternoon she sat in the corner of Noel's room and read aloud to him:

" 'Of all South American forest animals, sloths are the ones that live most completely in the trees. They have powerful claws, like hooks on the end of each leg, and hang upside down from branches, rarely, if ever, leaving the trees. They eat, sleep, mate and give birth in this position and have adapted to a completely arboreal life. Their fur grows in the opposite direction to that of most mammals, which helps the rain run off. They have extremely powerful limbs and are good swimmers, although they can only move awkwardly on the ground in a spreadeagled crawl. They also have very low body temperatures, which is why they are only found in the warm, humid tropical forests.' "

She looked up and was startled to find that Noel had moved. From his usual scraggy shopping-bag position he had let go with his foreclaws and was hanging by his back feet apparently staring straight at her.

She put the book to one side and walked over to him. Their faces were almost level. Out of a ruff of fur his blunt, good-natured face regarded her blankly. Upside down. The nose looked soft and velvety. Tommy resisted the urge to stroke it. The brown eyes blinked and the wide, comical mouth opened and closed without a sound.

"What are you thinking?" she asked. She caught herself waiting for a reply and laughed.

The whole point of getting the book out of the library had been to find out more about sloths as sloths and here she was, doing her mother's trick of pretending it was a little child.

Noel reached up with his forelegs and very slowly drew himself up into the branches. The interview or inspection or whatever it had been was at an end. In the upper tangle of branches was a shape that Tommy saw without noticing. A smooth, black, rounded shape.

She heard her mother shouting that tea was ready.

Halfway through the meal she suddenly sat bolt upright, nearly choking herself on a hastily swallowed mouthful.

"Eat more slowly," said her father. "You'll do yourself a mischief."

Tommy coughed and thumped her chest and drank a glass of water. The thing up in the high branches had suddenly jumped into her head and had revealed itself. It had been a violin case.

Chapter Four

"I'm going to strangle that paper boy," said Tommy's father.

"Girl," said Tommy.

"What?"

"It's a girl who delivers the paper. I saw her out of the window."

"What's that got to do with anything? I'm talking about the newspaper, not the boy or girl or whatever that delivers it." He threw the newspaper onto the kitchen table. "It's the wrong one."

Tommy looked at it. It certainly wasn't their usual morning paper. Their usual one was small and full of headlines and coloured photographs and special offers and games and quizzes. What had been delivered was one of those huge broadsheet newspapers with tiny writing and headlines like "Pound Down Against The Deutschmark" or "Floods In Bangladesh Leave Thousands Homeless".

Tommy's mother looked round from the sink. "I'll have a word with them. You can put up with it just for today, can't you?"

Tommy's father opened out the newspaper until it all but hid him. "How do I read this on the train?"

"Folded up, like other people," said Tommy's mother. "I'll phone the shop. No, hang on – isn't it the day for your magazine, Tommy? You could pop into the shop on the way to school. Tell them we got the wrong newspaper. Would you do that for me?"

"Yes. Okay." She got up from the table. "I'm just going to say goodbye to Noel."

Noel was slowly munching leaves. She stood underneath him. The violin case was gone – if it had ever really been there. Tommy was beginning to wonder. She had gone back into the room the previous evening after tea and looked up to the place where she thought she had seen it. Nothing. Just the hairy, leggy sloth hanging idly in the branches the way it always did.

Noel's head turned slowly and he looked at her, still munching.

"Goodbye," she said. "I'll be home about half past four. Be good." She was trying to think of something like: be good and I'll bring you some sweets, or be good and I'll buy you a present. But you can't really bribe sloths like that.

"Who put this back in here?" she heard her father shout as she headed for the front door. "Veronica, was this you?"

"Was what me?" from the kitchen.

"This plant."

"What plant?"

Tommy detoured into the front room. The large potted fern that had been exiled to the garden to make way for the hi-fi system was back in place. The black midi box had been shoved to one side and was half hidden by foliage.

"*This* plant. If you wanted it in here you could have *said*."

Tommy's mother came through, pulling her coat on. "It's nothing to do with me," she said. "Do you think I'd dare touch your record player once it was set up?" She

30

always referred to the hi-fi as a record player because it irritated him. She said it made up for all the things he did which irritated her.

"Well, it didn't *walk* in here on its own. It hasn't got *legs*, has it?"

"I haven't got time to worry about it now," said Tommy's mother.

Tommy's father saw her in the doorway. "Tommy?"

She shook her head. "Not me."

"It wasn't me or your mother. That only leaves you." Tommy knew this particular tone of voice from her father. It meant that nothing she said would be believed unless she admitted to the crime, whether she'd done it or not.

"Sorry," she said. She had no more idea how the plant had got back there than anyone else, but she knew that saying sorry would smooth everything over. Much easier than fighting it – which could lead to severe upheavals.

"Don't meddle without asking first," said her father. "You might have broken something. You're so thoughtless."

"Sorry," said Tommy again.

"Come on," said her mother. "It's no big deal. Time to go."

Her father continued to lecture her about her thoughtlessness all down the front path and along the road to the place where they went off in different directions. Her mother bibbed the hooter as she shot off in the car in a third direction.

It was an easy enough journey to school once she was on the train; and it was a pleasant surprise that Miss Scott had laryngitis and there wasn't a spare teacher to look after them for the last lesson of the afternoon.

Unexpected treats like that always brightened Tommy's day. She liked surprises. Like when Mr Ridley had got his fingers tangled up in the blackboard and had been carted

31

off to hospital gushing blood. Anything that made the day just that little bit special.

Like getting home at four o'clock instead of half past.

That was funny.

As she walked up the path to the front door she could have sworn she heard a piano playing. Not a record of a piano, or a piano on the radio – a real, live piano. Tommy could easily tell the difference. Recorded music had a different *shape* from live music. Recorded music was like spilled coins. Live music was plump and round and bobbed through the air like apples in water.

She turned the key in the lock and pushed the door open. The music had stopped. The big old house was completely silent except for the grandmother clock ticking to itself by the umbrella stand. The clock had a comfortable sound, like warm milk dripping into a mug. Clop. Clop. Clop. Clop.

Tommy threw her bag down and went into the front room. The piano lid was open and there was a thin book of music on the wooden, fold-out shelf on the front. Tommy tiptoed across the soft carpet, saucer-eyed and alert to the fingertips. Too surprised to be scared.

The room was empty. She touched a key and a low note rolled out into the still air. She considered burglars. *Piano-playing* burglars? She looked round and found nothing missing. She ran through the house but everything was as they had left it in the morning. Then she remembered Noel. A sloth thief. A wicked, piano-playing sloth thief.

Noel was midway between one branch and other, stretching a long limb and transferring his body in his usual slow-motion way.

Tommy gasped with relief.

"You're okay!"

Noel turned his curious, comical little face towards her.

She had never really noticed before the way his wide mouth seemed almost to smile. A very particular sort of smile. Not a happy-to-see-you type of smile, nor yet an I'm-having-a-nice-day kind of smile – more of an I-know-something-you-don't smile. But really, Tommy said to herself as she went back into the front room, *really* it's just the way his mouth *is*. Sloths don't really have knowing smiles on their faces any more than the expression on a cat's face is really smugness. It just looks that way.

Tommy looked at the music on the piano. Beethoven's Piano Sonata in C sharp minor. "Moonlight". She couldn't make sense of the dots and squiggles and splats. And as for "*Si deve suonare tutto questo ...* " It didn't even bear thinking about.

"I think," she said aloud, "I think this house is haunted." She particularly said it aloud so that if the ghost was nearby, it would hear her and know she wasn't afraid. "I think," she continued, looking slowly all around, "that there's a ghost here who plays the violin and who plays the piano and who prefers potted ferns to hi-fi systems."

But the ghost, if there was one, didn't do any of the things that ghosts do to let their presence be known. There were no knockings or rattlings or flying plates or unexpected coldnesses.

"It doesn't matter," said Tommy. "I shan't be frightened. I don't get frightened. But please, ghost, don't keep moving things around 'cos I get the blame. And Mum might believe in you but Dad *never* will. He's not the type. You'll never convince him you exist no matter what you do, and if you go around moving the hi-fi and bringing in plants that he's taken out he'll think it's me and I'll get into trouble. Ghost? Ghost, are you listening? You can play the piano some more if you like. I'll go and sit in the other bit of the room with my back to you if you're shy."

Tommy went and sat in her great aunt's wing-backed

armchair. She sat there quite still and silent for a long time but the ghost didn't come back to play any more of the Moonlight Sonata.

She didn't mention the ghost to her mother and father.

"You've found the key – that's good," said her mother.

"No," said Tommy. "I didn't actually. It came open on its own."

"It must have just been stuck," said her father, rather wishing that it had stayed stuck. "It probably hasn't been opened for years. The varnish gets tacky in the warm weather."

"Have you had a play of it, then?" asked her mother.

"No. Not yet. I shall, but not just yet." She wasn't sure whether the ghost would approve of her tinkling ineptly at the piano. It wouldn't if it had an ear for music, and she didn't want to upset it. Ghosts, she guessed, can probably get their own back in quite uncomfortable ways if you upset them.

"Did you see the man about the newspaper?" asked her father. He had drawn a lot of amused attention to himself that morning on the train, trying to find the sports page. Wrestling with unruly swathes of paper the size of small bedsheets did not fit into his idea of himself as a dignified Acting Deputy Chief Clerk. He did not intend that to happen again.

"I did," said Tommy, chewing a sausage and trying to remember exactly what was said. "The woman said that if you keep changing your order you must expect people to get muddled up."

"What's she talking about? No one changed the order."

"That's what she said," said Tommy. "She said first you sent in an order cancelling the paper that had been delivered here for years and ordering a new one, then you sent in another order for the original paper again."

"She's batty," said Tommy's father.

"It's just a mistake," said Tommy's mother. "Don't get in a twist about it." She looked at Tommy. "You sorted it all out, did you?"

Tommy nodded.

As she lay in bed that night she wondered whether the ghost had sent off the second order. If a ghost got used to a particular newspaper it might well get peeved at the appearance of a different one. Ghosts are probably quite conservative in their habits.

She dreamed that night that she was all alone in a big dark place and that someone was calling to her. The dark place was warm and she felt safe, but although she ran and ran after the distant voice, she couldn't find who was calling.

She woke up in the drowsy middle of the night and listened to the soft lilt of a faraway violin. This time she didn't get up or switch the light on. She just lay there listening until the dreamy music sent her off to sleep.

When she awoke in the morning she realised that she knew the voice that had been calling her in her dream.

It had been Great Aunt Tomasina.

Chapter Five

Tommy got into a new routine over the next few days. A damage limitation routine. It involved setting her alarm for ten minutes earlier so that she could get downstairs ahead of her parents and change back whatever the ghost had changed during the night.

Sometimes it wasn't much. The armchair might have been moved back to face the fireplace or an ornament could have been replaced when it had been put away – little things like that. And once she found that the television had been trundled to the french windows as if the ghost had planned on dumping it in the garden but hadn't quite got round to it.

The only thing these little changes had in common was that they were all attempts at getting the house back the way it had been before they'd moved in.

Things were moved during the day as well. The same sort of things. She never heard the piano being played again or found it open when she got home from school, but often things were shifted around as if the ghost had been making itself cosy.

She became convinced that the ghost was the ghost of Great Aunt Tomasina, come back to live in her old home and not approving of the alterations. Well – not come back to *live* exactly. Come back to ... dwell? ... reside? ... hang out ...? whatever ghosts do. Haunt, really, she supposed.

She wondered whether she should confide in anyone. There were two sides to this. One: no one would believe her, and if she insisted they'd think she'd gone potty or was moving things herself for a game. Two: they *would* believe her and they'd either move out or try to get rid of the ghost. And she didn't want to move – and even more than that she didn't want Great Aunt Tomasina exorcised. It was a problem.

During a free lesson one morning she asked Miss Scott:

"Do you believe in ghosts?"

"Well," said Miss Scott, "That's a good question." But instead of answering it herself she got the other children in the class to give their opinions. All the girls except one believed in ghosts, and about half the boys did. The girls generally thought ghosts were unhappy; the boys went on about them being violent and gory and dangerous.

Tommy's ghost didn't seem particularly unhappy – it didn't moan or anything – and it certainly wasn't dangerous, so their opinions didn't really help. Tommy's ghost was just *there*, quietly and patiently putting things back where it wanted them.

The only thing the ghost did that caused real problems was to keep sending notes to the corner shop changing the newspaper. Tommy's father thought someone was playing a stupid practical joke on him. Tommy fell under suspicion, but she denied it so vehemently that she was believed. In the end her father cancelled the order and bought his newspaper at the railway station.

Then something slightly unnerving happened. Nothing to do with the ghost – something quite different.

As Tommy came out of the school gates one afternoon she saw a tall, elegant man leaning languidly against the side of a tiny beetle-shaped motorcar, polishing his nails. It was Septimus Murgatroyd. At his side was a ragged heap in a rumpled raincoat – Alphonso Twigg, blinking through his glasses and wiping his nose on his sleeve.

Septimus Murgatroyd stepped forward, his hand outstretched.

"My dear young friend, how delightful to meet you again," he purred, smiling.

Tommy shook his hand. "Pleased to meet you," she said, lying. She looked up and down the road. There was a swelling tide of children and mothers all around her. "Did you come to see me?"

"But of course, my dear young friend." Smile. Smile. Smi-i-i-ile. "Didn't we, Twigg? Twigg?" Mr Twigg seemed in a trance. Septimus Murgatroyd kicked his shins. "The sweets, Twigg, you fool! The sweets!"

Twigg hopped about while he rummaged in his coat pocket.

"Frightfully nice day for the time of year," said Septimus.

Twigg pulled out a crumpled paper bag and waved it under Tommy's nose.

"A sweetie, little girl? Would you like a nice sweetie?" As nasal as an anteater with sinus trouble.

Tommy stepped backwards. "No, thank you."

Septimus Murgatroyd elbowed Twigg aside. "Of course not," he said. "What young lady of taste and refinement could possibly want a sweet from that revolting thing?" Smi-i-i-ile. "Might we offer you a lift home, my dear?"

"I don't get into cars with strangers," said Tommy.

Septimus Murgatroyd laughed a little too heartily. "But we're hardly strangers, are we? No, no, no. We're quite old friends, surely? I am, after all, your great uncle, aren't I?"

Tommy thought about this. Might it be rude to refuse a lift? She was on the brink of accepting when she caught a nasty gleam in Septimus Murgatroyd's eye. A nasty, hungry, impatient gleam that made her quite determined *not* to get into his little black marrow of a car.

"I still don't think I should," she said. "I'll have to ask my mum."

Septimus Murgatroyd pursed his lips and tilted his head thoughtfully. Suddenly Twigg popped round from behind him. "Come along, little girl, there's a good, nice, helpful little girl. Look at our nice motor car. Wouldn't you like to go for a nice ride in our nice motor car? A nice ride?" He blinked behind his glasses and oiled his hands together. "We'll give you money. Lots of money. Enormous amounts of … ooofffff … " Septimus Murgatroyd's elbow caught him neatly in the stomach, doubling him up.

Tommy gave the two of them a dubious look and walked rapidly away.

The last thing she heard from Septimus was: "You dimwitted scrag, why don't you learn to hold your tongue? You brainless bag of rags. Get into the car. I'll deal with you later."

She half expected to be followed, but when she glanced around the tubby little car was nowhere to be seen.

"I don't like the sound of that," said Tommy's mother. "What's he up to, offering you lifts? He's supposed to be living in the south of France. What's he still hanging round for?"

"I hope you were polite," said her father.

"Very," said Tommy. "But I didn't fancy getting into the car. It was the filthiest wreck I've ever seen. And falling to bits with rust."

"You did right, Tommy," her mother said. I don't like the idea of him lurking around. It's creepy."

"It *was* broad daylight," said her father.

"That doesn't make it any less creepy. He's after something, he must be. And that half-pint squirt that hangs around with him ... that Sprigg man ... "

"Twigg," said Tommy. "Alphonso Twigg. I think he's a bit ... you know ... loony. I don't think he's all there."

Tommy was on the lookout for the next few days but she didn't see her great uncle or the car although she did have a curious dream about them.

In the dream there was a tall tree outside her bedroom window. She dreamed that she woke up in the middle of the night and could hear Septimus and Twigg talking.

"Where's the jemmy, you tattered wreck?"

"Here. In my coat pocket, Septimus. I'll just ... "

"Careful, you fool – you'll have us out of this tree."

"It's got tangled in the lining. There ... it's free now ... "

"You poked me in the eye with it, you steaming clot. Give it to me."

"Sorry, Septimus. Here, I ... oh ... I've dropped it. Let go of my throat, Septimus, I'll climb down and get it." Then there had been a lot of creaking and rustling and a yelp from Twigg. "Help, Septimus! Help!"

And in her dream Tommy had got up and pulled the curtains and had seen Twigg hanging upside-down out of the branches, caught by his coat-tails and gibbering for assistance. And in her dream Tommy had laughed so much that she woke herself up, still laughing.

"I can't live with this kitchen any more!" yelled Tommy's mother one morning after spending five minutes trying to light the gas cooker. "I need some modern stuff in here or I'm going to freak out."

The following Saturday a van pulled up outside their

41

house and three enormous boxes were heaved off the back.

"I don't know how we're supposed to pay for this," said Tommy's father as they hauled the boxes into the kitchen.

"The same way we paid for your beloved record player," said her mother. "Monthly for the next two years."

The three of them set about the packaging and a cooker, fridge and a freezer appeared.

Tommy sat at the table popping the bubble-wrap while the kitchen was re-arranged around her.

Later on the man came to clean up Noel's room and Tommy's parents went out to attack the supermarket.

The sloth-man wore a flat cap and a brown waistcoat and had huge, gnarled hands. He was called Ted. He wasn't a full-time sloth-keeper, he told Tommy while she helped him rake up the old straw and put it in a black plastic sack.

"I used to be a park keeper," he said. "Until they retired me. Now I do a bit of all sorts. Hand me that shovel, lovey." He cleaned out the sloth-litter tray. The smell of the disturbed litter was overpowering, like a face-full of ammonia. "It's a good job the old chap only goes to the loo once a week," said Ted, filling the bag and tying the smell in with a length of twine.

Noel was dozing up in the highest branches.

"Funny old sort of pet to have," he said. He winked at Tommy. "Can't see you taking it for a walk."

"Not a very quick one, anyway," said Tommy. "Did you know they're in the same order of mammals as anteaters and armadillos?"

"I didn't. No, I must admit, I didn't know that." Ted opened the stepladder and started wiring the fresh branches up.

"Mmm," said Tommy, handing leafy branches up to him. "And they only eat the leaves and fruit of *one* particular tree. I read it in a book I got from the library."

"That so?" said Ted, his upper half hidden in greenery. "Just one tree, eh?" His face appeared. "It must be a pretty big tree, that, eh?"

Tommy grinned. "Not one *tree* – one sort of tree."

"Oh, I see."

"It's called ... oh ... I *did* know. A funny name. Beginning with C."

"Cecropia."

"That's it. You knew all along."

"Just teasing," said Ted, climbing down the stepladder and moving it along. "And did you know that the proper Latin name for him up there is *Bradypus infuscatus*? Poor little blighter."

"I think I'll carry on calling him Noel."

"I think you should. And did you know that greeny tint to his fur is algae?"

"What's that?"

"Like what you get in fish tanks. The green stuff that grows all over the rocks and glass inside fish tanks. But this one is a particular sort of algae that only grows on the fur of sloths. *Tricophilus welcheri*, they call it. Shocking name, isn't it? Pass up some more of those branches, will you, lovey?"

"How long have you been doing this?" asked Tommy. "I mean, how long were you helping my great aunt before we came along?"

"Oh, a few months. I'd do the cleaning up and that Hitch woman would stand over me with her notepad. Never liked that woman. There's not many people I can say that about. Most people's got something about them I like, but not that one. Cold as charity, that one. I could be cheerful as anything, whistling like a tree full of blackbirds, happy to be alive – and after ten minutes in a room with her it'd feel like a gloomy day in February."

43

"I know what you mean. she was my great aunt's nurse, wasn't she?"

"Not that I knew. That grand old lady didn't seem the type to me that'd need a nurse. Any illness come near her would be sent packing with a flea in its ear, I'd have said. No, that Hitch woman was here to study him up there, I was always led to believe. That was her job. Nurse your great aunt? I'd like to see anyone try." And he laughed – a lovely raucous, crackling sound.

"Funny thing is," he said a while later, "It's none of my business, but she had some strange characters round here while your great aunt was away. Staring up at Noel they were, one Saturday when I arrived. Staring at him and whispering. Funny pair of blokes."

"What were they like?" asked Tommy.

"One was a tall old chap – very smart – smarmy. The other was this little scruffy fellow with a squeaky voice. I saw them a couple of times. Pals of the Hitch woman, I suppose, although I never saw them before your great aunt went away."

Noel slept on, oblivious.

Full of puzzlement, Tommy helped Ted scatter fresh straw then stood waving at the gate as he drove off in his rickety old van.

Now what on earth had Septimus and Twigg been doing visiting the house while Great Aunt Tomasina was away? Visiting the house *before* the shipwreck? Visiting the house and whispering with the Hitch woman while they were supposed to have been living hundreds and hundreds of kilometres away in the South of France?

She was about to go back indoors when there was a honk and the sound of a car pulling up.

"Just the girl!" shouted her mother out of the car window. "Help us with the shopping, Tom-tom – we've got enough grub here to last us till the clocks go back."

Chapter Six

Do ghosts eat?
     This was a question Tommy found herself thinking about quite a lot over the following few days.

The war of nerves between her and the ghost had begun to wind down a bit. Fewer things were being shifted around – sometimes nothing at all, as if the ghost was gradually getting used to its house being reorganised and was minding the changes less and less.

But the arrival of the fridge and freezer shifted the focus of the ghost's activities from the living room to the kitchen.

Tommy would trot downstairs in the early morning to find the doors of both appliances wide open, and their contents strewn around the floor. She would get home from school to the same problem. It seemed only a matter of time before one of her parents would discover what was going on. And then what would happen?

But what worried Tommy more was that the ghost's new regime of disorder didn't seem to fit in with her belief that it was the spirit of her great aunt come home to roost. Great Aunt Tomasina's restless spirit might well fight against the old order of her home being disrupted, but was it really likely that even the *ghost* of a serious and sensible old lady would take to emptying out fridges and freezers?

Tommy felt her Great Aunt Tomasina's Ghost theory needed re-thinking.

But then something even more extraordinary happened.

She got home from school one afternoon to find that the ghost had been cooking. It was just after lunchtime on the afternoon when they usually did sport. Teacher shortages had struck again and they'd been sent home early.

A delicious smell wafted down the hallway as she opened the front door. At first she thought that her mother must have got home early and had decided to treat them to something special.

"Mum? I'm home. We got let off … "

No reply.

"Mu-um?" She went into the kitchen. It was empty. Empty of her mother, at any rate.

A couple of years ago her mother had set out on a health kick – aerobics, jogging, healthy eating. All that sort of thing. It had lasted about six weeks before her mother's natural inclinations had asserted themselves. The only relic of this fad was a cookbook called *The Gourmet Vegetarian*. Never used. Tommy's father swore blind he would actually *die* if he didn't get some sort of meat inside him at least once a day.

The Gourmet Vegetarian was propped open against the scales on the worksurface and scattered around it were dishes and measuring spoons and cups and knives and the chopped remains of a recipe for vegetarian ragout.

A place was laid at the kitchen table. A toureen of ragout steamed aromatically. A half-finished bowl sat on a place mat with a spoon still in it. A bottle of Mouton Cadet had been opened and a glass of the rosy coloured wine stood beside the bowl on a coaster.

Tommy slowly circled the deserted table. As if the half-finished meal wasn't bizarre enough, a well-thumbed paperback copy of *Anna Karenina* lay open next to the bowl.

This was very clearly not ghost-work.

"Mu-u-um?" yelled Tommy. "Da-a-ad? A-a-anyone?"

Aroma-filled silence greeted her call.

Whoever had cooked the meal, opened the wine and sat quietly reading *Anna Karenina* had obviously done a very swift vanishing trick on hearing her open the door.

Tommy had two choices. Either she could run screaming out of the house or she could search every room thoroughly. She picked up a broad-bladed kitchen knife. It felt strange and dangerous in her hand. She put it down again and armed herself instead with a large serving spoon. She would never have been able to use a knife, no matter who she found, but she felt she might be able to clout someone with the heavy spoon if the occasion arose.

She searched the house.

There was no one there. There was no sign of a forced window or anything. The back door was locked as ever and bolted from the inside.

She sat on the stairs. Perhaps it *was* her mother. Perhaps she had been sitting there eating and reading and had suddenly realised she needed something at the shops.

Tommy sat hopefully on the stairs for a quarter of an hour.

The front door remained closed. No one came back to finish their meal.

Deeply puzzled, Tommy went through to say hello to Noel. She always said goodbye to Noel on leaving the house and hello on her return, despite the fact that he was generally asleep.

He hung motionless, his eyes closed. There was that big, broad smile on his face. But that wasn't all.

Becoming suspicious, Tommy took the stepladder from its place by the door and opened it out under the apparently dozing animal. She climbed slowly and took a closer look.

There were food stains in Noel's tangled fur and a smear of ragout on his muzzle.

She stared silently at him for a minute or two, but he showed no sign of knowing she was there.

"Ahem!" she said.

An eye half-opened, then closed again. A long, slow tongue came out and licked the messy muzzle.

Tommy couldn't think of a single thing to say. As she climbed down the stepladder she thought she saw the smile broaden slightly.

She closed the door and stood thoughtfully for a few moments. She made going-away sounds with her feet then waited. After about five breathless, silent minutes she hurled the door open.

Noel hadn't moved.

"I'll catch you," she said. "Don't you worry – I'll catch you at it."

"That was very nice," said Tommy's father, pushing his bowl away. "Very gourmet indeed. What came over you?"

"I just felt like it," said Tommy.

"You can feel like it as often as you like for my money," said her mother. "I never knew you had it in you."

"I just followed the recipe," said Tommy. "It wasn't difficult."

"Try something with a bit of meat in it next time and it'll be perfect," said her father. "What's for afters?"

"Don't ask me," said her mother. "Ask the chef."

"I didn't do anything," said Tommy. "Sorry."

"There's a melon in the fridge," said her mother. "We'll have that."

Her father washed up. "Hello," he said. "What's this? *Anna Karenina*?" Tommy had left the book on the work surface. "Who's reading this, then?"

"Not me," said Tommy's mother. "You know I never get time for novels – I have enough trouble keeping up with the reading I have to do for work."

"We're doing it at school," said Tommy hastily.

"Really? Tolstoy? Good grief!" said her father. "You're certainly getting through it." Tommy had closed the book and had marked the place with a slip of paper. About a third of the way through.

"What's happened so far? asked her mother.

Tommy felt hot and cold at the same time. "Do you know the story?" she asked cautiously.

"Nope. Haven't a clue," said her mother. "You tell me."

Tommy folded her hands in her lap and leaned forward. "Well … " she said. "It's about this woman … called … "

"Anna?" said her mother.

"That's right. Anna. And she lives in this big house in the country with her mother and father and a mad old uncle and a stable full of beautiful black stallions. And she goes out riding a lot … and … and one day she loses control of her favourite horse and when it jumps over a gate she falls off … and … "

"Are you sure about this?" asked her father, who was reading the blurb on the back of the book. "It doesn't mention any of that here."

"I might have missed a bit," said Tommy.

Luckily for Tommy the doorbell rang. She decided she'd better get some idea of what went on in the book before they asked her again. She wished she hadn't said it was for school. Now they'd be on at her all the time about whether she'd finished it yet.

Her father went to answer the door.

"We were in the vicinity and thought we'd pay our

49

respects." The rounded, honeyed tones rolled down the hall. "I hope it's not inconvenient?"

Septimus Murgatroyd.

Tommy heard her great uncle and (presumably) Twigg being shown into the front room. Her father came into the kitchen wearing a harrassed face.

"What does he want?" mouthed her mother.

"How should I know?" whispered her father. "I'm not psychic. If I *was* we could have hidden under the table until they went away. I don't like unexpected visitors any more than you do."

"I *do* like unexpected visitors," murmured Tommy's mother. "Just not unexpected Septimus Murgatroyds."

"And unexpected Twiggs," said Tommy.

"Oh well, they're here now," said her father. "We'll have to make the best of it. Come on. Big smiles."

Septimus and Twigg were stooped by a glass-fronted cabinet, examining the contents and whispering.

"Ah, the lady of the house!" said Septimus, straightening up and offering his polished hand to Tommy's mother. "How delightful to see you again. And your little girl." Crocodile smile. "The little heiress. The young lady, I should say. The young lady of prospects. Yes, oh my, yes, quite the eligible young lady." He stared at Tommy. "I see you will be a great beauty when you grow up. I can see you'll turn a few heads."

Tommy seethed inwardly but kept her smile fixed. If I was older, she thought, and I didn't have to worry about what Mum and Dad would say, I'd tell him to get stuffed and kick them both out.

"I've never had the pleasure of seeing Tomasina's collection before," said Septimus. "Living abroad, you know, and having many things to occupy myself, I never quite got the time to visit." He sighed. "Sad to think that it was death that finally brought me here. I remember the deep shock I felt when the letter arrived informing me of Tomasina's death. I left my home immediately to see if there was anything to be done … but … " Another sigh.

Lying hound, thought Tommy.

"We were very close," continued Septimus. "When we were younger, you know. Tomasina and I, very close. Separated by time and circumstances." He seemed quite wistful, although his eyes never lost their gleam.

"She never mentioned you," said Tommy.

Septimus smiled. "Too painful for her, my dear young lady. Too painful. The parting of devoted siblings leaves a deep wound."

Load of old toffee, thought Tommy.

"Feel free to look round," said Tommy's mother, not meaning it.

"Really? Really? That would be most hospitable of you. My very good friend Twigg, here, is something of an expert in matters of antiques and curios."

"Am I?" said Twigg.

"Ha, ha!" Septimus put a long arm around the scrawny shoulders and squeezed Twigg like a nut in nutcrackers. "You know you are, my *dear* fellow." He smiled around the room. "So modest. So rich in knowledge and so modest. Don't you always find that with men of true ability?" He steered Twigg towards the cabinet that they had first been looking at.

Twigg writhed in his shabby suit. "Er … these … er … "

"Jade," said Septimus.

"Ah … yes … these jade pieces," said Twigg. "I couldn't help noticing them. Exquisite. Exqui-i-isite. If you were considering selling any of them, I'd … "

Septimus laughed loudly and unconvincingly, silencing Twigg. "You must forgive Twigg, he has no *tact*." Septimus spat out the word *tact*, glaring at Twigg, whose face crumpled into subdued silence. "Of course these dear people are not considering selling any of these delightful objects, Twigg. They are heirlooms." He smiled at Tommy. "Family heirlooms. You see," he rested his hand on Twigg's shivering shoulder, "we run a small antique shop. Twigg has always got an eye out for new things." The hand tightened its grip. "But we mustn't be over-acquisitive. There's a time and a place for everything, my very *dear* Twigg. A time and a place for everything."

"Sorry, Septimus," simpered Twigg. "I forgot myself."

"Would you like a drink?" asked Tommy's father.

"That would be very hospitable. Yes, yes, a small drink, perhaps. To oil the social wheels," said Septimus.

"We've got Scotch ... or brandy ... or some wine?"

"Wine would be a delight."

Tommy's father looked at her mother. "There's a bottle of Mouton Cadet somewhere, isn't there, dear?"

"I'll get it," said Tommy. "I know where it is."

"What a very good girl she is," she heard Septimus saying as she left the room. "An absolute credit to you. I can quite see why Tomasina should have chosen to leave the house in her competent hands."

Yes, thought Tommy, and the moon is made of green cheese.

She dug the bottle out of the broom cupboard where she'd hidden it. Only half a glass was missing. Carefully topping the wine up with tap water, she took the bottle through to the guests.

They were doing a tour of the room. Tommy wished they would have their drinks and go away.

Septimus seemed more interested in looking around the house and pretending he had never been there before.

They got the full guided tour.

"A delightful abode," said Septimus once they were back in the front room. "Quite enchanting."

"You haven't seen the best of it," said Tommy's father,

who'd had a couple of glasses of wine and was feeling more friendly. "You haven't seen our pet yet."

Twigg writhed on the couch next to Septimus. It was a little writhe, but Tommy didn't like it. There was something about it that made her think of a greedy child who's been told about a room full of sweets.

"A pet!" said Septimus. "How charming."

"I wouldn't call it charming, exactly," said Tommy's father, whose face was beginning to glow pinkly. "It's a sloth."

"Extraordinary," said Septimus. "A relic of one of Tomasina's travels, I expect."

"I suppose so," said Tommy's father. "I'll show it to you if you like."

"We'd be delighted, wouldn't we, Twigg?"

"Oh, yes. Delighted," said Twigg.

"If it's no trouble," added Septimus.

"None at all," said Tommy's father.

Tommy wished Noel hadn't been mentioned. She didn't want her great uncle and Twigg getting anywhere near Noel. Not after what she'd been told by Ted.

They went along to the glass room.

"There can't be many private houses with their own sloth," said Septimus as Tommy's father opened the door. "I trust it's securely locked in. It wouldn't do for it to be able to escape."

"He's *very* secure," said Tommy. "We look after him very carefully."

Noel was sleeping soundly and contentedly.

All the traces of ragout were gone.

Chapter Seven

"That was a turn-up!" said Tommy's father, closing the front door on their departing guests. "What did you make of that, then?"

"I thought it was a right cheek telling us that wine was naff," said Tommy's mother. "Cheek. Lacked body, indeed! Tasted watery. It tasted okay to me. Not that I drank as much of it as some people not a million miles away, and I shan't mention any names but watch my eyes."

"A couple of glasses," said Tommy's father. "That's all. Just to be sociable. Anyway, that wasn't what I meant."

Septimus and Twigg had shown a lot of interest in Noel. Tommy had watched them with deep suspicion as they pretended never to have seen the creature before. Noel hadn't shown any signs of life, although Tommy had had the definite feeling that he wasn't sleeping.

"Extraordinary animal," Septimus had said. "But not much of a pet for the young lady, I shouldn't imagine."

"I like him," Tommy had said. "I like him lots." She glanced over to Twigg, who had wandered to the back door and was apparently engaged in nothing more interesting than gazing out into the garden.

"He's no bother, I'll give him that," her mother had said. "It's like having a pet shopping bag."

Septimus had smiled (smirked?) at Tommy. "I'm sure you'd prefer a cat or a dog, though, wouldn't you?"

Tommy had thought about it. "As *well*," she had said. "Not *instead*."

Septimus had leaned over her. "Or a little pony all of your own."

"Yes," Tommy had admitted. "I wouldn't mind a pony."

Septimus had rested his hands on his knees and leant over till his long angular face was on a level with hers. "Strange as it may seem," he had said, "I happen to have an acquaintance who has a pony for sale. The dearest, sweetest little pony you could ever imagine. With a muzzle like velvet and a mane like spun sugar. And eyes that are great black pools. The sweetest-natured pony that ever a young lady could wish to ride upon. And he loves to be ridden and there's no one to ride him now because my acquaintance's daughter has grown too big and doesn't love it any more."

Tommy had looked at her great uncle, wondering why she was being told all this.

"Nice pony," Twigg had chimed in. "A nice, nice pony. Such a nice pony."

"We couldn't afford it," Tommy's mother had said.

"Ah!" Septimus had lifted a long, smooth finger. "But this acquaintance of mine is looking very particularly for an arboreal animal for his nature park. And it struck me as I first looked at your friend the sloth up there that it was the very sort of animal that my acquaintance wants. Now, isn't that a coincidence? Now, my dear, if you knew your sloth was going to a home where he'd be happy and contented and well looked after, wouldn't you be happy to swap it for a lovely little pony that hasn't a friend in the world, and desperately needs a pretty and intelligent young lady to care for him? Mmm?"

Tommy had glanced up at Noel. One eye had been half open. She could have sworn he had shaken his head.

"Sorry," Tommy had said. "The pony sounds lovely, but I couldn't swap Noel for anything."

"Not even to make a beautiful, sad-eyed pony the happiest pony in the world?"

"No."

"We can't get rid of the sloth anyway," Tommy's mother had said. "It was in the will that we had to look after him. Don't you remember?"

Septimus had straightened up. "No one need know," he had said. "I can't imagine anyone would check up on you. And the sloth would be *very* well looked after, I can assure you."

"Would you like a pony?" Tommy's father had asked.

"Yes. I would," Tommy had said. "But not instead of Noel. Thanks for the offer, but I'm not letting Noel go for *anything*."

"We could give you money," Twigg had said.

"Twigg!" Septimus had hissed. "Don't be so indelicate. If the young lady doesn't wish to exchange her sloth for a pony then the matter is closed. I must apologise once again for my friend Twigg. He had a curious upbringing, you must understand. Snatched from his cradle by a family of peripatetic stockbrokers. Very sad. He doesn't always appreciate how normal people behave. He doesn't always appreciate the niceties of a situation. Twigg, my dear friend, isn't it time we were leaving for that appointment?"

"Appointment, Septimus? What appointment?"

"That *very particular* appointment which we have this evening," Septimus had said. "Surely you remember? Our *appointment*?"

"Ohh. Ahh. Yes. The appointment. The very particular appointment. I remember, Septimus, of course I do. I remember. With … um … with … "

"Professor Pretorious of the National Institute," Septimus had said.

"Yes. Protessor Prefforious ... yes ... how could I have forgotten?"

"How *could* you?" Septimus had said.

He had bundled Twigg out of the room.

Septimus's parting words had been: "If you *do* change your mind, Twigg and I are staying at the Bide-a-Wee Boarding House in Froggett Street. We shall be there for a few weeks yet."

"You're not going back to the south of France yet?" Tommy's mother had asked.

"Not just yet. We've a little business to clear up first."

And they had gone.

"And," said Tommy's mother as they went into the front room, "I didn't believe all that old guff about an appointment, either. I reckon they just turned up to have a nose around."

"I wouldn't let him have Noel if he offered a million pounds," said Tommy.

"What were they up to?" said her mother thoughtfully. "I don't like it."

"Don't start getting silly," said her father. "I don't think they were up to anything."

Tommy's mother looked at him. "You're wrong," she said. "And I won't feel happy till I know they're out of the country. Especially that slime-ball Twigg."

Tommy wondered whether this was the time to tell everything she knew. No, not yet. Not just yet.

"I think I'll go to bed now," said Tommy," "To read for a bit."

"Your book's on the worktop, don't forget," said her mother.

"Oh, yes. Thanks."

She picked up the book and went through to say

goodnight to Noel.

"There you are," she said to him. "I didn't sell you, did I? Or swap you for a pony. I hope you're grateful." The sloth hung with its eyes closed. She couldn't tell whether he was asleep or just faking. "Especially as I've got to read this rotten book now. And it's all your fault." She came up right underneath him. "I know it was you doing all that in the kitchen," she said. "It's no good pretending you can't hear me. I *know* it was you. And I bet it was you doing everything else as well."

Silence.

"You might as well admit it," she said. "I shan't tell anyone else."

She gave Noel half a minute to respond, but he didn't.

"Oh, be like that, then."

She left him to it and went up to bed.

The book was dreadful. Page after page of sentences that went on and on and on, without anything happening. And then she realised that she'd only been reading the Introduction and hadn't even started on the proper story yet.

In the dreamy moments before falling asleep she wondered what her great uncle had actually meant when he'd asked whether Noel was kept securely.

Tommy was on the train on the way to school the next morning, trying to sort out her books and things without taking them out of her bag. There was all the usual mess: pens and screwed-up tissues and erasers and half a packet of mints and a couple of bits of broken ruler and various scrunched-up sheets of paper. And one neatly folded piece of paper that she didn't remember.

She pulled it out and unfolded it.

"*Anna Karenina*," it read. The words were written in meticulously neat handwriting. Beautiful handwriting that curled and flowed across the page with those broad lines and slender lines that come from using a fountain pen.

"The tragedy of a woman who leaves her husband for another man … "

It was a brief synopsis of the plot of the book.

It was open question time at the end of the afternoon.

Tommy threw her hand up. "Miss? Can animals think?"

Miss Scott rocked back on her desk, supporting herself on her arms. "Nice question, Tommy. Can animals think? Well, they certainly have brains and a level of capacity to think, but not in the way that humans do. I mean, cats know when it's dinner time and know that fires are hot and rain is nasty and wet. So we have to assume that there's a thinking process going on in their heads … "

"Can animals learn to read, though?"

The rest of the class laughed. Miss Scott smiled. "I don't think any have yet. It's a very complicated thing, reading. You probably don't realise how many different things your brain has to do in order for you to read. You have to have a language … "

"Moo!" shouted someone. "If cows wrote things down, miss, it'd all be moos, wouldn't it?"

This idea went through the class and everyone started making their favourite animal noises. Tommy sat patiently in a tide of barks and grunts and neighs and squawks and meows.

"Supposing," she went on, once the fun had died down, " … supposing there was an animal … an unusually *clever* animal that learned to … *do* things. Like, learned to read and cook and play the piano … " More laughter. Tommy persisted, raising her voice above the noise. "What would people do if they found out about it?"

"Tom-tom's got a cat that plays the piano," yelled someone.

"Settle down," said Miss Scott. "That's a perfectly reasonable question. What do *you* think would happen to such an animal?"

"They'd take it away and experiment on it, miss," said someone. "Wouldn't they?"

"They'd stick it in a zoo," said another voice. "So everyone could see it."

"No they wouldn't. They'd put it on telly."

The argument bounced around the classroom. But Tommy had already heard enough. She imagined Noel being taken away by a lot of nosey, interfering scientists and put in a locked room and made to perform for them. *That's* what would happen. And Noel knew that's what would happen. That was why he indulged himself when he thought there was going to be no one about.

The question was, the *big* question was: did Great Aunt Tomasina know about it?

Tommy couldn't wait for the lesson to end so she could get back home. She was sure Noel trusted her a little bit. Her task now was to convince him she was *completely* trustworthy.

As she walked through the school gates she heard animal noises behind her. A gang of her classmates were standing laughing, obviously at her. They had always thought she was a bit odd. Now they thought she was completely batty.

"Going home to play chess with your cat?" someone shouted.

"Get stuffed!" yelled Tommy, without bothering to look round.

"Moo!" said someone.

Tommy halted, turned and advanced on them with a fierce look on her face.

They scattered. Escaping from the loony girl with the weird ideas.

Chapter Eight

Tommy ran like mad to the station and managed to catch an earlier train. It trundled along so slowly that she began to jig up and down on the seat to try and urge it on. A woman was sitting opposite. She frowned at her over her newspaper. Tommy took no notice. Come *on*, train! I want to be at home. I want to make sure Noel's safe.

"Will you keep still?" said the woman.

"Sorry. Sorr-ee," said Tommy sharply, not in the right mood for that sort of thing. "I wasn't doing it to annoy you."

"Well it did," said the woman coldly.

" 'Scuse me for breathing," said Tommy. "Anyway," she stood up, "This is my stop."

"You're a very rude young girl."

Tommy opened the door a centimetre as the train slowed. "Would you have said that if I was three metres tall and had a machine gun?"

"I beg your pardon?"

Tommy jumped off and hared up the platform. She came round the corner of her road at a trot then stopped, hidden behind the bushes until she got her breathing under control.

Instead of going in through the gate she clambered onto the low wall and pushed herself between the bushes and the brick pillar in the far corner of the front garden. She crouched, listening. She crept across the narrow bit of grass so that she was under the bay window. Now she could hear it.

She lifted her hands on to the windowsill and gradually raised her head. It was no good. The combination of the net curtains and the high-backed sideboard with the plants all over it made it impossible to see what was going on in the room. But the piano was being played.

She crept to the corner of the house and climbed on the wall. She got a leg over the side gate and heaved herself over, landing on all fours on the gravel path that ran down to the garden.

Her heart beating very fast, she slid round to the french windows. She could hear the piano much more clearly now. She was almost frightened to look. She took a deep breath. She sidled round the corner of the house and looked in.

Noel was at the piano, his long legs hanging, his body swaying slightly and his head tilted to one side, a beatific smile on his face and his eyes closed in rapture. He was playing Beethoven's Moonlight Sonata.

He was playing it beautifully.

Tommy didn't know what to do. She didn't want to frighten him. She stood staring through the window, listening to the gentle music and watching the long, ungainly arms with the hooky claws moving over the keyboard.

After a while the music came to a perfect close and Noel's arms dropped. Spontaneously Tommy began to clap. Noel's head snapped round. There was a flurry of greeny-brown fur, all arms and legs, and he was off the piano stool and out of sight.

Tommy unbolted the side gate and made her way round to the front door.

She went straight to Noel's room.

He was hanging innocently from a branch. He might have been there all day, being a simple, snoozing sloth. Except that he hadn't.

Tommy stood underneath him. "You play very well," she said.

Noel's eyes were tightly closed.

"Couldn't you teach me to play like that? I shan't tell anyone."

Silence.

"Thanks for the rundown on that book. I'd have cracked up if I'd had to read it all. They liked the meal, by the way. My mum and dad. I pretended I'd cooked it. They were amazed. Perhaps you could show me how to cook like that as well. I'm not going to *tell* anyone about you, you know. You *can* trust me. Noel, for heaven's sake – I *know* you're not asleep. I just *saw* you."

She might as well have been talking to an ordinary sloth for all the response she got.

"Oh, all right," she said. "If you don't *like* me. I'll still look after you like Great Aunt Tomasina asked me to. And I *won't* tell anyone about what you get up to. Just don't make so much *mess*, please."

As she turned towards the door she heard a snapping sort of sound.

She spun round. One of Noel's arms was stretched towards her, a single claw beckoning. He'd snapped his claws to get her attention the way a person might snap their fingers. He was looking at her with that same secretly amused smile on his face.

She stopped beneath him. The claw rose and patted her head.

"Can't you speak?" asked Tommy.

Noel shook his head.

"Can't you make any sort of noise at all?"

Noel's arm doubled up on itself and he scratched thoughtfully at his nose with one outstretched claw.

"I was … ' The claw rose to silence her. Then Noel folded his middle claw under, stuck the other two claws in his mouth and emitted a shrill whistle. *Wheee-ooo-eeeee!*

Tommy laughed. Noel lifted his head and gave a little shrug as if to say "it was nothing".

"Where do you come from?"

Noel hung himself upside down by the back claws. He shaded his eyes with one claw and pointed with the other.

"You mean a long way away?"

He nodded.

"South America?" Noel looked carefully at her then tapped his wrist with his claw.

Tommy was puzzled for a second then: "Oh, you mean what time is it? We're safe. No one else will be home for ages." The next thing she knew there was a long hairy arm around her neck and Noel was transferring his weight on to her. She clasped her hands under him.

He tapped her shoulder and made an impatient gesture towards the door.

"You're a weight," she said. "That's what comes of nicking grub out of our fridge instead of sticking to your leaves. I hope you're not planning on me carrying you all over the place."

Three claws drummed rhythmically on her shoulder.

She lugged him out into the hall.

"Where are we going?"

Noel pointed up the stairs.

"I can't carry you up there. You're too heavy." Noel stretched out an arm, caught a banister rod and swarmed up the banisters. "you're only supposed to be able to move at two kilometres an hour," said Tommy, running up the stairs to keep up with him.

On all fours, he scuttled across the landing and into the room that had been Great Aunt Tomasina's study. They hadn't decided what to do with the room yet. It was a terribly serious sort of room – terribly academic. Filled with shelves that were filled with books, and with filing cabinets filled with files and card-index boxes filled with index cards. There was a large old desk with a clattery old typewriter on it, a blotter, a pen holder, an in and out tray.

On the only available bit of wall space was a map of the world with little flags stuck in it to show where Great Aunt Tomasina's travels had taken her. The map was festooned with flags like bank holiday bunting.

Noel's claws latched on to Tommy's arm and he towed her over to the map. He clambered up her body and pointed to South America. Venezuela.

The next question that came into Tommy's mind wasn't an easy one to put into words. "Are you an ... *ordinary* sloth? I mean – can all sloths do what you do?"

Noel shrugged, climbed nimbly over her shoulder and down her back.

"Do you mind!" said Tommy. "I'm not a trampoline."

Noel waved a dismissive claw and shambled over to the desk.

"It's no good," said Tommy. "It's locked and we don't know where the key is. Mum's been searching for days. She's planning on getting a locksmith in. I don't ... "

Tommy's eyes weren't quick enough to see where it came from as, with a flourish, Noel lifted an arm with a key gripped between two claws. He obviously knew of some secret recess undiscovered by her mother.

He opened the bottom left-hand drawer and rummaged.

The drawer was filled with small hardbacked notebooks, green with red trimming, battered and tattered and stained. Some of them looked very old.

Noel pulled one out and gestured for Tommy to join him on the floor.

She sat cross-legged and he dropped the notepad into her lap.

Venezuela: The Rain Forests. In large oval handwriting – Great Aunt Tomasina's handwriting. It was dated the previous year. Noel prodded Tommy's arm and waved a claw to get her to open the notebook.

"Yes, yes. All right. For heaven's sake," said Tommy," 'You're so *impatient*. I don't *believe* you. Who ever heard of an impatient sloth?" He drummed his claws on her knee.

She opened the book.

It was a diary. A daily chronicle of events written in various pens and pencils. Sometimes the writing was quite neat, and on other pages it was scatty and smeary and covered in stains.

Noel nudged Tommy's hand aside and clawed through the pages. He tapped at an entry and Tommy began to read.

" 'Extraordinary,' " she read aloud. " 'An extraordinary day by any standards. It started with a puzzle and ended with astonishment. When I woke up I noticed that the bag with my travelling books in, which was by the tent-flap, had been disturbed. At first I thought some creature of the forest had nosed into it. My copy of *Jude the Obscure* was missing. I made a mental note to keep the tent flap securely, tied in future. During the afternoon I was investigating the fauna of a large cecropia tree when I came across the most incredible thing. So incredible that I can still scarcely believe it. High in the branches I discovered a specimen of *Bradypus infuscatus* apparently engaged in reading my copy of *Jude the Obscure*. Hanging by three legs and holding the book in its fourth, it was, as far as I could make out, so deeply absorbed in Thomas Hardy's prose that it had not heard my approach. Sloths are noted for being deaf, so this did not surprise me. Sloths are *not*, however, noted for their appreciation of literature. Upon seeing me, the sloth dropped the book and pretended to be asleep. I tried, without using undue force, to bring the creature down out of its tree, but it proved immobile.

" 'Overwhelmed by the experience I descended to give this more thought. Later in the day I climbed up again with my copy of *Middlemarch*, another book which I always take with me on my adventures. I propped the book in the branches near the sloth and went back down to ground level. I await events with eager interest.' "

Tommy turned the page.

" 'An unforgettable day. I am calling the sloth Noel because it will be Christmas in a few days. I awoke and got out of my tent to find Noel hanging in the lowest branches, holding out my copy of *Middlemarch* with a look of evident satisfaction on his face at having finished it so quickly. He cannot speak but appears to have perfectly developed reasoning facilities. He can clearly read English, and is also capable of writing it, although this is a slow and very laborious process for him due to the difficulty he has in holding a pen. His writing style is, however, exquisite. He understands spoken English. Of course, my first question was how he learned these skills. His written responses to my questions show that he has no memory of having been taught these things. It seems to pour out of him quite naturally but with no explanation. He has no memory of ever meeting any other human being except myself. It is an unfathomable mystery. I intended to retrace my steps and return to England in a very few days, but I could not live with myself knowing I had left such a profound enigma behind me. I shall have to give this a lot of thought.' "

Tommy looked at Noel.

"You really don't know how you got to be able to read?" she asked.

Noel shook his head.

"Weird."

Noel nodded and shrugged. The sound of the front door being opened echoed up the stairs. Noel streaked across the room and out of the door like a greeny-brown comet.

"Tomm-mmy?"

"Mum. I'm up here." Tommy put the notebook back in the drawer and closed it.

"What's this?" called her mother. "Nothing cooked for us today? You're slipping."

Tommy stepped out onto the landing.

"I haven't had time." She ran downstairs. "Mum? How long do sloths live?"

"I haven't a clue."

"I hope they live a long time. I want them to live for years and years."

Chapter Nine

There was no way Tommy could get to sleep that night without another look in Great Aunt Tomasina's notebook. Fortunately her mother and father slept in a room right at the front of the house, while Great Aunt Tomasina's study was only a short hallway off from Tommy's bedroom at the back.

She could hear the faintest tones of the violin as she crept out of bed and pulled her dressing gown over her pyjamas. The violin just *had* to be Noel, although she was intrigued by where he could have hidden it. Once out of her room and tiptoeing along the hall, she found herself in complete silence. She walked carefully with her arms outstretched. She didn't dare turn on the hall light.

She went softly into Great Aunt Tomasina's study and closed the door. She had thought about going and getting Noel, but all that moving about in the middle of the night might wake her parents up, and she didn't want *that* happening. She trusted her mother to keep the secret but her father was one of those people who would feel he had to *do* something. Tell the proper authorities, or something like that. One thing Tommy was sure of was that if Great Aunt Tomasina had wanted the "proper authorities" or whoever to know about Noel, then they would already know about him, which they obviously didn't. And Noel wasn't going to get sold out by Tommy if she could help it. No way.

She closed the heavy velvet curtains and switched the light on. She felt brave and daring and ever so slightly wicked to be up and investigating all alone in the middle of the night. But the room felt friendly, as if it liked her. As if it knew she didn't mean any harm.

She drew out the Venezuela notebook, quickly found the place and started reading again.

"I shall have to retrace my steps to Guanare in the very near future as my supplies are running dangerously low. Noel has stayed with me and is at this moment hanging from the roof pole of my tent reading the *Mill On The Floss*. It is an excellent book and I am sure he will enjoy it. I can't help thinking I would find my travels less strenuous if it were not for all the books I need to carry with me. However, as I cannot conceive of a trip undertaken without George Eliot in my backpack I shall have to endure the burden of literature as stoically as I can. Thank heavens for paperbacks, I say!'

The next entry read: 'I have explained to Noel that I have to go and he has made it very clear to me that he wishes to go with me. I got out my folding world map to give him some indication of the distances involved. So far as I could make out, he seems to understand. I would not normally even consider removing a creature from its natural habitat, but I have given a lot of thought to the Noel question and I am convinced that it would not harm him if I took him home with me. I hope I am not making an error. One thing that I am quite certain of is that Noel will not become an exhibit or a *cause célébre* in England. I shall give him as good and fulfilling a home as I can and learn from him all that he is willing to reveal of himself."

The next few pages chronicled Great Aunt Tomasina's journey down the River Guanare, and the 400-kilometre drive to Caracas, where she spent Christmas Day. Then, as Tommy read, she and Noel took an aeroplane to England and arrived home on New Year's Eve. And at that point the notebook ended.

Tommy ferretted through the drawer, trying to find a follow-up book that would tell her what had gone on between Great Aunt Tomasina's return and her decision to travel to Bhajangaya. But the drawer had no such book in it.

Tommy searched the rest of the desk and eventually found a notebook with the current years' date on the cover. she read for a solid half hour and uncovered the following tale:

Noel continued to perform miracles. Great Aunt Tomasina installed him in the conservatory at the back of the house (The Glass Room) and arranged for a man to deliver food and keep his room clean. She discovered he could play the piano. Mozart, Beethoven and Chopin were his favourites, although he also loved to play pieces by Gershwin and Cole Porter. Having three claws instead of five fingers, he had to adapt the more complicated pieces. This he did brilliantly. He also played the violin – Mozart and Beethoven again. Great Aunt Tomasina had bought him sheet music. He rapidly took to Brahms but hated the more modern stuff. He read a lot of philosophy and positively devoured the classic novels. He would read the newspaper avidly. He would cook delicious meals which they would eat together, although the trouble he had with holding cutlery made him a messy sort of dinner partner. He had a fondness for brandy and good wine, although never in excess.

But still, while his abilities continued to reveal themselves almost daily, Great Aunt Tomasina was completely unable to help him remember *where* his talents and knowledge came from. A few friends and neighbours became aware of Noel's existence, but Great Aunt Tomasina never breathed a word about how unusual he was.

Instead she wrote cautious letters to various experts, asking about animal prodigies. Replies came back telling her about chimpanzees who had vocabularies of fifty or more words, and of parrots that communicated their wants by pressing coloured buttons or of dolphins that performed extraordinarily complicated tasks. But none of them read books, played the piano or cooked gourmet meals.

"I have one last hope," Tommy read. "A very good friend of mine from my college days, Esme Phang. Professor Phang now. When she retired from her Chair at University she upped sticks and went to live a life of contentment and meditation in a small town named Bhajangaya in the foothills of the Himalayas in Northern Nepal. She was a brilliant scientist, far ahead of her time. Her speciality was the brain, or rather, the mind. She isn't contactable by normal methods so I shall have to seek her out in person. But this means I shall have to leave someone to look after Noel. Ted is very good, but I need someone who can live in. It is a pity little Tomasina is too young, or I think she would be the perfect person. I have high hopes of Tomasina."

Tommy re-read this passage a number of times. I have *high hopes* of Tomasina. That was *her*. Her great aunt was writing about *her*. *High* hopes. Waaahhh!

"I have engaged a woman named Unity Hitch. If she proves reliable I shall tell her about Noel and leave him in her charge when I depart for Nepal."

The next few pages were about Great Aunt Tomasina's preparations for her journey. More ominous to Tommy was an entry which read: "I am not easy in my mind about Unity Hitch. She is a cold creature. Very efficient, but somehow lacking those qualities that would have made me wish to confide in her as to Noel's capacities. Nevertheless, the time for me to set off is drawing close, so she will have to be trusted to some degree. I hope I am not making a mistake."

The last entry was as follows:

"Today I set off for Nepal. I have told Unity Hitch that Noel is unusual, but not the extent of his unusualness. I have also asked Noel not to reveal himself to her. I think this is safest. I hope that Esme Phang will be able to help Noel and provide the key that will unlock his past. I have a feeling this may be my last great adventure."

Tommy closed the diary.

"I have a feeling this may be my last great adventure." She wiped a tear from her cheek.

Suddenly she wanted to see Noel. Not for any particular reason. Just to see him. She switched the light off and glided silently downstairs and round to the back of the house.

As she approached Noel's room she heard strange noises. Not the violin, but thuds and rustlings and a hissing voice saying "Let go, damn you! Will you let go!"

She didn't pause. She thrust Noel's door open.

A figure had hold of Noel and was trying to drag him over to the open back door that led to the garden. Noel was clinging grimly on to anything within claw-reach with three arms and hitting the would-be kidnapper over the back and head with the violin.

The figure was swathed in a black cloak with a deep hood over its head.

"Leave him alone!" shouted Tommy.

The head jerked up and the hands lost their grip. Noel ploughed up through the branches and continued to rain blows on the hooded head from a safe height.

With a screech of frustrated anger the figure made a dive for the door. Tommy ran and caught hold of the trailing cloak. Quite what she would have done if she'd managed to keep hold of the kidnapper, she couldn't have said, but the sloth-burglar was so intent on escape, that rather than turning to give her a bashing, it put all its energies into pulling away from her while at the same time attempting to shed the encumbering cloak.

The figure ran off into the night, across the garden and out of sight; but in those few moments before the darkness engulfed him, Tommy knew beyond any doubt that he was none other than Great Uncle Septimus's slimy little sidekick, Alphonso Twigg.

Chapter Ten

"What's going on?"

Tommy looked at the scrap of paper on which Noel had laboriously written his question. Something suddenly dawned on her, which she should have guessed some time ago. Noel hadn't a clue what was happening in the house. It was hardly surprising, really. Who would dream of going into a greenhouse inhabited by a "pet" sloth and tell him what was going on? People are supposed to tell all the house secrets to their bees, and cats and dogs would find out just by being in the rooms where things were being discussed. But poor old Noel, shut away in his back room, hadn't been told anything since Great Aunt Tomasina had left for her tragic journey to Nepal.

The most difficult bit was explaining that Great Aunt Tomasina was not coming back. Not ever.

Noel climbed slowly up into the topmost branches. Tommy stood looking up at him for a few moments. He obviously wanted to be alone.

"I'll look after you," said Tommy. "I'll make sure they don't get you. I'll think of *something*."

She didn't like the idea of leaving Noel on his own. Twigg might be lurking somewhere. She closed and bolted the outside door. She remembered how Twigg, the evening before last, had stood by the door. He must have disengaged the bolt then – planning on coming back at dead of night and spiriting Noel away while the household slept. She dug out a huge adjustable spanner from the cupboard under the stairs. She made herself as comfortable as she could, wrapped in Twigg's discarded cloak and settling in a nest of straw in the corner of Noel's room. She sat watchfully with the spanner clutched in both hands, waiting for a sound or a shadow from outside the black wall of glass.

She woke up in a blazing shock of sunlight. Noel was shaking her. Memories of the previous night came at her in a stampeding herd.

Noel was tapping at his wrist. She didn't have a watch on. She didn't have a clue what time it was. She tottered out into the hall. The grandmother clock showed half past six. She rubbed her eyes, feeling shivery and blurry and all out of shape.

She went upstairs and crawled into her bed.

There was so much to think about. It was getting out of hand. She couldn't cope, but she couldn't think who to share the secret with. Her brain wheeled and whirled like a merry-go-round that gradually slipped out of focus and drifted off into the emptiness of a shallow, fitful sleep.

"Tommy! For heaven's sake. Look at the time."

Tommy blinked blearily at her mother. She had slept through her alarm. She felt as if her entire body were made of stone and didn't want to be moved. She'd turned into stone during the night. Very achey stone.

Her mother leaned over her. "Tommy? Are you okay? You look dreadful."

Tommy managed to dredge an arm up from under the blankets and catch hold of her mother's hand. Her mother sat on the edge of the bed. She stroked her forehead.

"Don't you feel very well, darling?"

Tommy didn't have to pretend. She felt awful. It wasn't a tummyache or a headache or a cold, or *anything* in particular. She felt as if someone had taken her plug out and drained all the life out of her.

"I don't think you ought to go to school," said her mother.

Tommy smiled weakly.

"Now I *know* you're not well," said her mother. Tommy usually did cartwheels if she got a day off school, even when she was ill. It was generally worth having a cold to spend the day in bed reading and being looked after. A big jug of lemon barley water and a thermos of soup. Bliss.

Her mother tucked her in, cocooning her in blankets. "You get some sleep," she said. "I'll pop up again in a few minutes."

Tommy woke up at half past eleven, feeling much better.

There was a tray by her bedside. A jug of fruit juice, a thermos (probably the soup), a bowl and a spoon, a plate of chocolate biscuits and a box of tissues. And a note: "I'll try to get back a bit earlier. Stay in bed and keep warm. Love, Mum." and "Hope you feel better soon. Ring one of us at work if there are any problems. Dad."

She had a glass of juice, a bowl of soup (thick vegetable) and a few biscuits. Then she drew the curtains and saw that the garden was dancing with sunlight.

She got dressed then ran down to check on Noel. She had a moment's panic on finding his room empty, but then she heard a shrill whistle from the front room and found him there in the wingback armchair with his hind claws up on the footstool and his blunt nose in a book.

She knelt by the chair. "Good, is it?" she asked.

He nodded and showed her the cover. "Flaubert," it said. "*Madame Bovary*."

"I've never even *heard* of Madame Bovary," said Tommy, wishing she had. "Is she good, then?"

Noel gave her a slow, unfathomable look.

"What?" said Tommy. "*Now* what have I said?"

Noel put the book down and patted her gently on the head.

"I don't know how anything so small can be so patronising," she said. "I've got the day off school. I felt really *ill* earlier. But I feel fine now. Shall we do something together? I mean ... what do you normally do?"

Noel shambled over to the drinks cabinet and took out a bottle of brandy. Her father's special Christmas brandy. It was half empty. Noel waved the bottle at her, and gestured to the book and the piano.

"I see," said Tommy. "You loaf about having a good time."

Noel took the cork out of the bottle and sniffed. An ecstatic look came over his face.

Tommy took the bottle out of his claw, re-corked it and put it in the cupboard.

"No," she said. "That's *not* what you're going to do." She thought for a minute. "I know," she said. Noel had sat himself down by the drinks cabinet with his arms folded and a sulky look on his face. "You can teach me how to cook. I could make something really nice for when Mum and Dad get home." Noel gave her an unimpressed look out of the corner of his eye.

"You're just like my dad," she said sternly. "Now stop it. I can't stand sulking. Let's go and cook something." She went into the kitchen, sat down and waited.

A few minutes later Noel came ambling in. He'd have had his hands in his pockets if he'd had any pockets to put his hands in.

"Finished your sulk, have you?" asked Tommy.

Noel gave her a disdainful look.

"Why do you think those people are after you?" asked Tommy.

Noel shook his head and shrugged.

"They must know about you," said Tommy. "About the peculiar things you can do. It's that Hitch woman, I bet. Great Aunt Tomasina was dead suspicious of her, you know. I reckon she's told them about you being different and they want to take you off and ... I don't know ... " The things her school mates had said came back to her, but she didn't think it would be very tactful to mention zoos and scientific experiments or things like that to Noel " ... well ... take you off ... " she ended.

Noel gave her an alarmed and affronted look.

"Don't worry," she said. "I won't let them. I saved you last night, didn't I?"

Noel nodded and patted her arm.

"But I can't keep saving you. I wish there was someone I could trust. I wish I could trust Mum not to tell Dad. It wouldn't matter about Mum knowing, but Dad would go to the police or something, and if they caught my great uncle or the Hitch woman and they told them that you could play the piano and things they'd probably *still* take you away." Tommy sighed. "I wish Great Aunt Tomasina was here. She'd know what to do. I wish I didn't have to do this all on my own." She sank her chin in her hands.

Noel gave her a comforting pat on the shoulder then trundled off to the shelf with the cook books.

He opened *The Gourmet Vegetarian* in front of her.

"Don't you eat meat at all?" she asked.

Noel frowned and shook his head.

"Dad prefers meat."

Noel tapped at the open book. A recipe for vegetarian goulash.

"Yes, okay," she said. "Vegetarian, then." She read the list of ingredients and they set about finding them in the cupboards and vegetable rack. They assembled everything they could find but there were still a few things missing.

"Can we do without them?"

Noel shook his head.

"I'll have to go down the shops, then. Good job I've been saving my pocket money. I hope it's not going to be too expensive. Will you be all right while I'm gone?"

Noel nodded.

When she got back he was already at work mixing and dicing. He also had a glass of her father's brandy at his side.

"I thought we weren't going to drink any of that," said Tommy, dumping the carrier bag on the table.

Noel waved a claw at her.

"He'll go spare when he finds it all gone. He's not going to believe it evaporated, is he? He's pretty dim, but not *that* dim. I wish you'd think about *me*."

Noel carefully picked up the glass and upended it into the mixing bowl. He gave her a complacent look.

"Yes. All right. I'm sorry. I thought you were drinking it. I'm sorry."

Under Noel's guidance Tommy prepared the rest of the ingredients. He let her do all the work, sitting comfortably on the work surface with his back to the wall, nodding or shaking his head to her questions, windmilling his arms to show her what to put where.

Onions began to sizzle in the pan. Noel crossed one leg over the other and rested his arms across his stomach. Next time Tommy looked he was fast asleep.

Tommy finished the cooking, creeping round the kitchen and scraping pans as quietly as possible so she wouldn't wake him.

After about half an hour the goulash was ready for the oven.

"Ahem!"

Noel slumbered on.

"Ah-*hem*!" She tapped a spoon on the work surface. Nothing. Not a glimmer. She banged the spoon on the surface.

Noel opened one eye.

"It's ready," she said. "Thanks for all your help."

Noel spread his arms. The spread turned to a stretch and he yawned. He rippled his claws up and down in the air. He kicked the cooking debris out of the way and clambered into Tommy's arms.

"What?"

He rippled his claws in the air again and pointed to the living room.

"You want to play the piano?"

He nodded.

"Will you teach me something?"

Nod.

She carried him through to the piano. He opened the lid of the stool and rummaged through the papers.

"Something simple," said Tommy. Noel pulled out a booklet: *Christmas Carols: A Beginner's Guide to the Piano*.

She flipped through it. "Good King Wenceslas". "Silent Night". "Away In A Manger". "Oh, Come All Ye Faithful". It looked pretty straightforward. There were none of those clusters of notes on the staves that she'd seen on the Beethoven piece he played.

"Not really very summery, are they?" she said. He snatched the booklet away, crammed it back into the stool and shut the lid. "No, no! Don't be like that. I'd like to learn them. I'd like you to teach them to me. I just thought something a bit more seasonal might be better."

Noel shambled over to the french windows, his back to her.

She opened the lid and took out the booklet again. She opened it at "Silent Night" and sat at the piano. She glanced round at him. She pressed a note. *Doing.* "That's C," she said. "I know that much." Very slowly and laboriously she tried to work out the melody. "Si-i-lent-t … night … ho-oly … night … a-all … is … " A shrill whistle stopped her. She looked round. Noel had his claws over his ears and a pained expression on his face.

He climbed up her leg and sat in her lap.

He played the carol easily and perfectly. He pointed to the words printed above the staves.

"You want me to sing?"

He nodded.

Noèl accompanied her while she sang. She wasn't too sure to begin with, but soon she was singing at the top of her voice, thoroughly enjoying herself.

She didn't hear the front door open. She didn't hear it close, or hear footsteps coming down the hall.

" … sleep in he-eavenly pea-eace! slee-eep in he-e-e- … '

"Tommy!"

The front room door opened and her mother stood staring in the doorway.

Chapter Eleven

"Now start again ... from the beginning."
Tommy shifted uncomfortably on the couch. Noel sat in a neat little bundle by her side, arms folded elegantly on his stomach, claws interlocked.

Her mother was sitting on the arm of the wing-backed armchair, smoking her first cigarette in twelve years. At her feet were Great Aunt Tomasina's notebooks, open at the relevant pages.

"He plays the piano?" said her mother.

Tommy nodded.

"And he cooked that meal we had the other night?"

Nod again, not sure whether to smile or not. Tommy's mother looked as if she needed a blanket throwing over her and ten or eleven cups of hot sweet tea inside her. She glanced uneasily at Noel. Noel raised an arm and wriggled his claws at her. She went pale and took a long drag on her cigarette.

"I'm ... a bit ... " She looked at Noel, then at Tommy, then back to Noel. He was smiling at her.

"Yes," said Tommy. "I know. So was I."

"It's quite ... unusual ... isn't it ...? I mean ... very ... um ... "

'Unusual?"

"Yes."

There was an anxious silence. Noel slid down off the couch and went to the drinks cabinet. He poured a glass of brandy and held it up for Tommy's mother.

"Thank you," she said. He raised his eyebrows and did one of his "It was nothing" shrugs. She drank the brandy in one swig and spent a long time coughing.

"And you think Murgatroyd and Twigg are after him ... trying to kidnap him?"

"And the Hitch woman," said Tommy. "And I don't think they are – I *know* they are."

"Why didn't you tell me before?"

"Because I thought you'd tell Dad."

There was a knowing silence between mother and daughter.

Noel refilled her mother's glass and filled one for himself. Tommy frowned at him. He fluttered a claw over his heart. He was in shock as well and needed brandy – that's what he was telling her.

"We've made a nice meal," said Tommy. "Vegetarian goulash. It only needs putting in the oven."

"I came home early to see how you were," said her mother blankly. "I took a half day off to look after you." She looked down at Noel. He patted her knee reassuringly and wriggled his eyebrows. "Oh ... dear ... " she said. "Your father will ... "

"You mustn't tell him. Mum? You won't, will you? You know what he's like."

"But ... "

"Great Aunt Tomasina said I was to look after Noel. Didn't she? In her will she specifically said to look after him. And we said we would. We signed things and everything."

"Yes. But we hardly ... I mean ... " She glanced

88

nervously at Noel, who was beaming up at her. " ... I mean, no disrespect, but you're not quite what ... we ... were ... expecting."

"That's no excuse," said Tommy determinedly. "I'm not going to have Dad send Noel off to be ... to be *anything*. Noel's staying here – with us." She looked pleadingly at her mother. "He's nice, he's really nice. He's my best friend. Dad won't have to know. You'll keep him secret, won't you?"

A long worm of ash fell from her mother's cigarette. Noel lifted the edge of a rug and brushed it underneath.

Tommy's mother laughed breathlessly. Tommy smiled.

"I suppose," said her mother, "Your father doesn't have to know *everything*. But what about Murgatroyd and the others? We've got to do something about them. I'm not going to be able to sleep at night knowing that little fiend Twigg is lurking about outside. I mean, let's be sensible about this."

"We could set a trap for them," said Tommy. "Something like ... like ... one of those noose-things hidden by straw that when they step into it whips them up into the air upside down. And then we could bash them." Noel nodded, making fierce bashing motions with his arms. Bash. Bash. Bash.

"I'm not sure that comes under the heading of being sensible about it," said her mother. "I was thinking more along the lines of phoning the police."

"You can't. They'll take Noel away."

"I don't see why they should. We needn't even mention ... Noel ... Oh dear, I wish your great aunt was here. I'm hopeless at things like this."

"That's how I felt," said Tommy.

Her mother stubbed her cigarette out in a saucer and looked at the clock. "Your father will be home in a minute. Come on, Tommy, what do we do?"

Tommy stood up. Suddenly the indomitable spirit of Great Aunt Tomasina seemed to have flowed into her. She felt very strong and positive and determined.

"Right," she said. "First of all Noel can sleep up in my room with me. I'll keep my door and window locked so he'll be completely safe. Dad's got a driving lesson tonight, hasn't he? So while he's out we can go over to that guest house where Murgatroyd and Twigg are staying. We can tell them we know what they're up to and that they're to stay away or there'll be trouble. We can tell them we'll get them locked up. And if they do tell anyone about Noel we can just deny it. Say they're potty. No one will believe them, and Noel's good at looking ... looking like an ordinary sloth when he wants to. And then they'll go away – back to France or wherever. *That's* what we'll do."

"Veronica – test me."

"I haven't got time. This report's got to be in first thing tomorrow."

Tommy's father stood in the middle of the front room. "My driving test is on Friday," he said loudly to the room in general. "And no one will help me with my *Highway Code.*"

"Give it here," said Tommy.

"Thank you," said her father, giving her mother a disdainful look that reminded Tommy vividly of Noel.

"Right," said Tommy. "Tell me ten things that you should do when driving in fog."

"Ten?"

"All right. Five."

"Slow down."

" 'Check your mirrors and slow down,' " read Tommy.

"Yes. Yes. I know that."

From the far side of the room, from under a pile of documents, came her mother's voice. "Always check your mirror before you do anything."

"I'm going to fail," said her father. "I can't stand it."

"They don't fail you on the *Highway Code*," said her mother. "If I were you I'd concentrate more on driving in a straight line."

A hooter sounded from outside. The final driving lesson.

Tommy and her mother gave him five minutes to get clear before they locked the house and set off for Froggett Road and the Bide-a-Wee Guest House, to confront Murgatroyd and Twigg.

It was a double-fronted house with a neon sign over the door: VACANCIES.

They went into the hall.

"Hello?" shouted her mother. "Anyone here?"

Tommy spotted a bell and pressed it. A tiny, fluttery old woman appeared.

"I'm so sorry to have kept you waiting – Mr Possit's got one of his necks on him and I haven't had a minute all day. Have you booked?"

"We don't want a room, actually," said Tommy's mother. "We're looking for a Mr Murgatroyd."

"Mr …? Oh – you mean Professor Murgatroyd. Oh yes, we're *very* proud to have him staying with us. It's always nice to have a professional man in the house. Raises the tone so – and he is *so* charming."

"Professor?" said Tommy.

"Yes indeed. An eminent scientist." She glanced up at them. "A *research* scientist. Such a lovely man. So cultured – so … oh … so … " Words of praise seemed to fail her. " … so knowledgeable."

Tommy and her mother looked at each other. "I don't suppose you know exactly what he *does*, do you?" asked her mother.

91

"He *researches*," said the little old woman proudly, basking in the glory of having him under her roof.

"Into what?" asked Tommy.

The old woman blinked at her. "Oh, something *important*, I'm sure. He did mention it. He's such an interesting man to talk to. Oh – I remember – yes – he works for a large cosmetics firm. He's one of those people who makes sure that all the new cosmetics that come out are safe."

Tommy's hair all but stood on end. "He's one of those people who put chemicals in rabbits' eyes!" she shouted.

The old woman looked affronted. "I'm sure he doesn't do things like *that*," she said. "Not a nice man like *him*. The very idea!"

"Is he at home at the moment?" asked Tommy's mother. Her voice had gone very steely. The sort of voice she saved for people who were going to get into trouble with her.

"I believe he is. Room number seven. Shall I call him for you?"

"No," said Tommy's mother. "It would be much more of a surprise for him if we just went up, if you don't mind."

"Well … I'm not sure … "

"We're related to him … distantly." Tommy's mother smiled. "Wouldn't it be more fun to just go up and surprise him?"

"Oh … yes … I suppose so. You will knock, won't you? He's probably busy. I shouldn't like him to be disturbed."

"We won't disturb him any more than is necessary," said her mother.

They went upstairs.

Room seven. Tommy's mother knocked and threw the door open in one movement. Murgatroyd was bent over a desk with a scalpel in his hand. There was a board on the desk, and on the board was pinned a mouse. Pinned on its back by all four paws and neatly cut open down the middle.

Murgatroyd bounced out of his chair and put himself between them and the murdered mouse.

"My dear ladies ... " he said. "My very dear ladies ... how ... how *nice* to see you."

"Don't count on it," said Tommy's mother, "*Professor*."

The oily smile fixed on his jaws and his eyes darted from Tommy to her mother.

"How can I help you?" he asked. There was blood on his fingers. Tommy felt like running at him and pummelling him with her fists.

"You can explain what that slime-ball Twigg was doing in our house last night, for a start," said Tommy's mother.

He spread his hands innocently, noticed the gore on his fingers and quickly put them out of sight behind his back.

"I know nothing of that," he said. "I haven't seen Mr Twigg for a couple of days. Did he call on you, then, without my knowledge?"

"Let's stop playing games, shall we?" said Tommy's mother. "I'm not going to bother asking you what you want Noel for. I've got all too good an idea of that already. We came here to tell you that if we find you or that Twigg-creature within half a mile of our house again we're going to call the police."

"My dear lady ... "

"You're horrible!" shouted Tommy. "People like *you* ought to be put on boards and cut open."

"Really, now let's be sensible about this – emotional responses are very unreliable ... " He advanced on them. "I will admit that in my anxiety to study your slo – Noel ... I may have misled you slightly ... "

"Slightly?" yelled Tommy. "You want to cut him up, you monster!"

Murgatroyd smiled. "No, no, no, my very *dear* young lady. You've got hold of quite the wrong end of the stick. I wouldn't *dream* of doing any such thing with ... Noel. I merely wish to study him. You do know, do you, that he is a quite remarkable creature? Think of the advances that science could make by a thorough study of such a creature. Think of the benefits to mankind. Look, I shall be open with you. I am in a position to offer you a large sum of money – a very large sum of money – if you will release Noel into my care. He will be well looked after, I assure you. He won't suffer in the slightest." Murgatroyd puffed himself up to his full height. "I run the largest and most up-to-date laboratory in the country. My work is done for the good of mankind."

"Hogwash!" said Tommy's mother. "You people are all the same – meddling and interfering. Poking into things you should leave alone. You *enjoy* it. And you pretend to be helping humankind. You disgust me."

Murgatroyd's smile faded and his eyes went hard and cold. "Disgust? Disgust? *I* disgust *you*? That is typical of your sort. You understand *nothing* of what goes on. Someone has to do this work. What would you say if you bought soap that raised blisters on your skin and used shampoo that made your hair fall out? How else are we to make sure the products you buy are safe other than by testing them on animals?"

"The same way we did *before* your sort started experimenting on animals. People washed before the likes of you came along – people kept their hair clean before all you scientists started cutting animals up. That's just an excuse, and I'm not prepared to stand here listening to you. I'm telling you, keep away from our house and keep away from Noel."

"This is foolishness," said Murgatroyd in a last attempt. "I can offer you *thousands* of pounds. Think what you're turning down – *thousands* of pounds."

Tommy screamed and rushed at him. Her mother managed to grab her collar and pull her back. Murgatroyd looked quite shocked. He pointed a shaking finger at Tommy. "I shouldn't mind experimenting on you, young lady," he snarled, all trace of urbanity gone. "I shouldn't mind getting *you* in my laboratory."

"Right," said Tommy's mother, keeping hold of her with some difficulty. "That does it. I'm calling the police." She turned and walked out of the room, dragging the livid Tommy along with her.

"I'm a very important man, I'll have you know," shouted Murgatroyd as they went down the stairs. "I'm not just *anyone*."

The little old woman was standing in the hall, looking very anxious.

"I hope you haven't upset the professor," she said nervously.

"I hope we have," said Tommy's mother. She slammed the front door behind them and looked down at Tommy. "Well," she said, "I hope that's sorted *him* out."

Tommy looked at her. "Where do you think Twigg was?"

They stared in horror at each other then ran for the car. Where was Twigg?

Chapter Twelve

Tommy's mother halted the car in a screech of brakes and they pelted up the path. Everything looked normal. Everything looked just as they had left it. As they closed the front door they heard a series of shrill whistles from the back of the house.

They ran in a panic to Noel's room. But Noel seemed to have things perfectly under control.

Twigg was hanging upside down in Noel's room with a loop of rope around his ankles. His coat hung over his head as he revolved slowly on the end of the rope. Noel was hanging by two claws from a branch and lazily kicking at Twigg to keep him spinning.

There was a broken pane of glass by the bolt and the back door was open.

"He-elp ... " came a thin, miserable voice from under the flaps of the coat. "Help me-e ... ouch ... he-elp ... "

Noel grinned at the two and waved a triumphant claw.

Tommy looked up at him in admiration. "That was my idea," she said. She looked at her mother. "And it worked."

Noel nodded and gestured to the apparatus he had assembled. It was quite simple. He'd found a coil of rope in the cupboard under the stairs. He'd made a noose out of one end (like Tommy had suggested), then he looped the rope over a high branch and had knotted the other end to a particularly heavy branch. He'd covered the noose with straw (as Tommy had said) and had released all but one of the chains holding the hefty branch in the air.

An unsuspecting Twigg had broken a pane of glass (obviously) and released the bolt. He had opened the door and stepped neatly into the hidden noose. Noel had undone the last chain, the heavy branch had fallen to the floor and Twigg had been upended with both ankles tangled in the noose.

"Right," said Tommy's mother, pushing her sleeves up above her elbows and advancing on the inverted Twigg.

"He-e-elp ... "

She unbuttoned his coat and his ferretty face appeared. He wasn't any prettier upside down than he was the right way up. His hair was standing on end and his face was bright red. He waved his arms uselessly and blinked at them. The collar of his shirt was up (down?) around his mouth.

" ... He-elp ... "

"I'm sorry we weren't in when you called. Did you want anything in particular?"

" ... He-e-e-e-elp ... "

"Tommy, would you like to go into the kitchen and get our biggest carving knife, please?"

" ... He-e ... eh?" Twigg's eyes went round. "I ... wasn't ... excuse me ... I knocked ... but ... " He tried a little laugh and gulped loudly. "I don't think ... you ... I ... " He began to wriggle. "Don't carve me up! You mustn't carve me up ... Help! Help! They're going to carve me up – He-elp!"

"Quiet, for heaven's sake," said Tommy's mother. "I've never met such a weed in my life."

Tommy stepped right up close to Twigg. "Tell us what you were planning on doing. Otherwise I'm going to go and get that carving knife and chop you into little pieces."

"She will, you know," said her mother. "She's completely uncontrollable when she loses her temper."

"And you needn't lie," said Tommy. "Because we've only just come back from beating your boss up. They were carting him off to hospital when we left, so if you don't want to join him you'd better tell us *everything*!"

Noel lowered himself down onto Tommy's shoulder and gave Twigg's nose a tweak with his claw.

"And there's more where *that* came from," said Tommy as Noel snapped his claws in Twigg's face. "Now. Who are you and what are you up to? And how does that Hitch woman come into it?"

The story as Twigg told it didn't come out very coherently. He had to be poked and tweaked and urged on before they finally got the full tale out of him.

It went as follows: Despite Great Aunt Tomasina's attempts at concealment, Unity Hitch had very quickly begun to suspect that there was more to Noel than she was being told. She had at one time been an assistant in the laboratory where Murgatroyd worked and was aware that Murgatroyd's particular field of interest was something called behaviourology. Murgatroyd, by the way, was not his name – his real name was Pretorius. Behind the fairly reasonable sounding title of behaviourology was hidden a whole host of misery and animal abuse. Throwing dogs into steep-sided tanks of water to see how long it took them to drown. Doing things with cows' brains and monkeys' brains and sheeps' brains. Horrible, horrible things that Pretorius would write up into papers which he would publish and be congratulated on.

Now Hitch knew very well that Great Aunt Tomasina would never allow someone like Pretorius within a hundred miles of Noel. She also knew that Pretorius would pay her a lot of money to get at Noel. Simply stealing Noel and handing him over wasn't practical – Great Aunt Tomasina was far too canny to allow that to happen. So Great Aunt Tomasina's trip to Nepal was a god-given opportunity – especially if she *never came back*. Hitch contacted Pretorius and The Plan was worked out.

This part of Twigg's story chilled Tommy and her mother to the marrow. Great Aunt Tomasina was to be murdered and Pretorius was to pose as her long-lost step-brother. He would claim her Estate, as her only living direct relative, and the Estate would include Noel. All quite straightforward and legal. Except for Great Aunt Tomasina's will, which upset everything.

"And what's happened to the *real* Septimus Murgatroyd?" asked Tommy. "Did you kill him as well?"

"Oh, no. Oh, no, no, no. Not at all ... not in the least. We found him living alone in a tiny village in the south of France. Quite isolated ... completely harmless. No newspapers or television or anything. He doesn't even know his step-sister is dead." Twigg brightened up a little. "He wasn't a problem ... we didn't have to do *anything* to him."

"But you killed Great Aunt Tomasina?" said Tommy, her eyes blazing.

"No. Not *me*. Not *me*. It was Pretorius who was behind it all. I didn't do anything – hardly anything at all." His face crumpled. "I'm really not very good at this sort of thing. I wanted to be a vet, you know. I love animals ... " He gave Noel a mangled grin. "I've always been kind to animals ... nice animals. Nice little animals." He frowned. "But Pretorius is so ... *difficult*. He gets angry very quickly, you know. Very quickly. You wouldn't believe it. He's a very violent man if he's crossed. It wasn't *my* fault. I'm only a humble assistant. All I do is clean beakers and sweep the floor. It's not my fault."

"Oh, shut up!" said Tommy's mother. "Tommy, watch him. I'm going to phone the police. They'll know how to deal with all this."

Tommy's father was in a daze. He had come home from his driving lesson to find a police car outside and Tommy and her mother giving statements to two police officers inside. Twigg had already been taken away for questioning. Tommy and her mother were careful to say nothing to anyone about Noel's special abilities. Apart from that they told the police everything.

"I don't understand," said her father.

"No," her mother patted his knee. "Of course you don't. There's some supper waiting for you in the kitchen. Why don't you trot off and eat it, eh?"

Her father wandered out, looking bewildered.

The police thanked them and left. Murgatroyd, or rather *Pretorius*, was to be picked up that evening and an all-points bulletin went out about Unity Hitch. They'd have her in no time, they said. No time flat. And then the full force of British justice would come clanging down on them like a steam-hammer.

Tommy and her mother nailed a piece of plywood over the broken pane in Noel's room and made sure the door was firmly bolted, just in case. It had been a long day. Noel hung sleepily from a high branch. Tommy's father watched them from the doorway.

"All this for *him*?" he said, looking at Noel.

"Apparently," said her mother.

He shook his head. "What's so special about *him*?"

"Does he *look* special to you?" asked Tommy's mother.

"No. Not in the least."

"Well then," she said. "There you are." She banged a

final nail in the plywood. "I think we all ought to go off to bed now. I think we've done quite enough for one day."

Tommy lay in bed. Sleeping wasn't easy after all the excitement. Very faintly she could hear a violin playing – a slow, sad lament. Noel was playing a funeral song in remembrance of Great Aunt Tomasina.

Tommy wiped tears out of her eyes and curled up.

It seemed outrageously unfair to Tommy that she should be expected to go off to school the next morning as if nothing had happened. She switched on Breakfast Television to see if there was anything on the news about it. It wasn't even mentioned. Not a word. Someone in the Royal Family had tripped on a kerb and had stubbed their toe. The television studio was full of experts: a paving stone expert from the local council; a toe expert who put everyone's minds at rest about how quickly the injured royal person would be back on their feet; an historian who pointed out that down the years many generations of the Royal Family had hurt themselves in similar ways, and that most of them had gone on to be useful and admirable monarchs. There was a Royal horoscope, a Royal recipe and a lot of photographs of fat Royal babies. There was nothing about Great Aunt Tomasina's death or the hunt for or capture of the evil Professor Pretorius and his sidekicks.

Tommy's father seemed equally indifferent. He roamed around the house, reading from the *Highway Code*. " 'If you are riding or herding animals after sunset, you should wear light-coloured or reflective clothing and carry lights which show white to the front and red to the rear,' " he announced.

"But supposing they *haven't* been captured?" Tommy

pointed out to her mother. "Supposing they're still out there, waiting for us all to go out so they can come in and get Noel? Think how you'll feel if you get home this afternoon and he's gone."

"You're not having the day off," said her mother. "And that's final. Anyway, Noel seems perfectly able to look after himself." She glanced at her husband, who was pacing the hall, muttering:

" 'When driving in fog, it is vital that you should obey the rules in Rule 55.' What's Rule 55? I don't remember Rule 55. Veronica, what's Rule 55?"

"How on earth should I know?" shouted her mother. "You've got the book."

"But you're a driver," he said, frantically ferretting through the book. "You must know."

"It's probably something about not driving indoors at night without displaying a fog-duck in your windscreen."

"Fog-duck? Fog-duck? What's a fog-duck?"

"David, will you calm down? There's no such thing as a fog-duck. I was joking." She looked wearily at Tommy. "He's going to drive me barmy. I know what'll happen now. He'll get in a panic and start babbling in the test about fog-ducks, and they'll never let him within fifty yards of a car again for the rest of his life."

Tommy went out into the hall. "Have you thought about a push-bike instead?" she asked her father.

"You're ruining my concentration," he said. "You do know that, don't you?"

"It was just a thought."

Her mother stood behind her. "Come on, David – it's time for work. Put it away and forget about it until tomorrow. If you don't know it now you never will."

Tommy went in to say goodbye to Noel.

"Now you be super-careful," she said. Noel nodded and did some practice karate chops with one long arm. "That's it," said Tommy. "If anyone comes for you give them a good bashing. I'll get back as early as I can. You'll be okay, won't you?"

Noel nodded, made bashing motions with his arm and drew a claw across his throat to signify that anyone who fancied trying to kidnap him would find themselves having a pretty rough time of it.

Tommy gave him a final anxious look as she left the room.

He grinned at her and did an upside-down he-man pose, hanging by his feet.

She smiled and waved goodbye. She felt it was going to be a very long day.

Chapter Thirteen

B y the time Tommy got home that afternoon she had convinced herself that she would confront a disaster. At one end of the scale she imagined Pretorius & Co. jacking the entire house up, loading it on to the back of a lorry, and dashing up the motorway, screeching with triumphant laughter, trailing furniture and ejected items of Great Aunt Tomasina's collection. Lower down the scale of horrors she imagined the house ransacked and Noel vanished who knows where. Even at her most hopeful she dreaded to find a Noel-shaped emptiness in the house.

It was with some relief that she found him brooding over the chessboard.

"Any trouble?" she asked breathlessly, having run all the way from the station.

Noel waved an impatient claw for silence, without looking up. She stood watching him, getting her breath back.

"I—"

He brandished a claw and frowned at her.

She sat down and waited. After about five minutes he moved a knight and leaned back with his arms folded and a satisfied look on his face.

Tommy looked at the muddle of pieces. She had never understood chess.

She looked at him. He gave the chessboard a sweeping gesture and grinned at her.

"Did you win?" she asked.

He nodded.

"Am I allowed to talk now?"

He nodded again and began rearranging the chess pieces to their starting positions.

"Has anything happened?"

He shook his head and gestured for her to sit opposite him. "I can't play, you know," she said.

When her mother got home he was still trying to explain how the various pieces moved around the board. Tommy couldn't have cared less, but Noel wouldn't let her just give up and wander off.

"Is there anything you can't do?" asked Tommy's mother.

Noel rubbed his chin then opened and closed his mouth a few times.

"He means he can't talk," said Tommy.

"Thank heavens for that," said her mother. "He looks the sort that would never shut up."

Noel gave her an affronted look and turned his back on her.

"I've been on the phone to Stingemore – remember?" said Tommy's mother. "The solicitor. I told him that the bloke he thought was your great aunt's step-brother was a complete impostor. I asked him what sort of proof of identity he'd asked for. He said his secretary had dealt with all of that and he'd have to look at the files. I told him not to bother. I also told him not to try and lay his own incompetence at someone else's door. I asked him what he intended to do about it. He said Pretorius could be done for fraud and that he'd set the wheels in motion immediately."

"So Pretorius will be put away, will he?" asked Tommy. "For a long time?"

"If they catch him."

"If? What do you mean, if? Didn't they get him last night?"

"Apparently not. I phoned the police this afternoon. Apparently he did a bunk from the guest house right after we'd left."

"And what about the Hitch woman?"

"Nope. They haven't got her either. No one seems to know where she is. She could be anywhere."

"Oh, brilliant!" said Tommy. "So what do we do now?"

"Sit tight," said her mother. "Keep our eyes peeled, lock up and wait for news. What else?"

What else, indeed?

Tommy had another one of her strange, vivid dreams that night. She dreamed she was woken up at dead of night by very loud violin music. Not Noel's usual classical-sounding music, but a wild country-dance type music. She crept downstairs to Noel's room. She opened the door and found Noel and Great Aunt Tomasina engaged in a frantic, stomping dance. The curious thing was that she wasn't surprised. It all seemed perfectly normal to her and all she was worried about was the amount of noise they were making. She was afraid they would wake her mother and father.

Great Aunt Tomasina was singing in time to the thudding of her feet. "Take your partner by the claw, spin him round towards the door, tuck up your petticoat, stamp your shoe, grab your sloth and doosey-doo … "

"Sshhh!" hissed Tommy, waving her arms. "You'll wake everyone up."

"We're having a last dance!" shouted Great Aunt Tomasina, "They're coming to take him away tomorrow. Hitch and the Professor – sure as ninepence." And they twirled together as if their lives depended on it.

One thing was for certain. Mad as the dream might have been, it was definitely a warning. A warning for Tommy that Noel would be in danger that following day. Sure as ninepence. Tommy got up, determined not to go to school. She knew it would be pointless arguing the toss with her mother. Her best chance was to pretend to set off, then sneak back. There'd be trouble on the following Monday, but it would be worth it if she saved Noel from being abducted. You have to take risks sometimes.

Her father was like an octopus with St Vitus's dance. Reading manically from the *Highway Code*, he buttered an envelope and dipped a corner in his boiled egg.

"David," said Tommy's mother patiently, "You're eating the gas bill."

His driving test was at noon. If he made it to noon. He looked nervous enough to shake himself to pieces before then.

Tommy's mother straightened his tie and patted his hair flat. "Don't worry about it."

"I'm not. I'm not worried at all," he said, trying to clamber into Tommy's school blazer. "What makes you think I'm worried?"

Tommy's mother helped him off with the blazer and tucked him into his own jacket. "Oh, nothing," she said soothingly. "Nothing at all, really. It was just a faint impression I got, that's all." She did up his buttons. "Now," she said. "You know what train to catch back so you're in plenty of time?"

"Yes. Yes. Of course. I'm not stupid. Oh, no! What order do traffic lights change in? I've forgotten. I can't remember a thing."

"Red. Red and amber. Green. Amber. Red," said Tommy.

"Is it? Are you sure?"

Tommy nodded. "Certain."

"Now," said her mother, "I'm leaving the car for you. It'll be outside in the road. Can you remember that? You've got the keys, haven't you? And in case you lose them or eat them or have them stolen by aliens, there's a spare set in the drawer in the cabinet in the hall. Have you got that?"

Tommy's father nodded. "But what if … "

Tommy's mother pointed to the front door. "Go to work," she said. He went, muttering to himself about box junctions.

Tommy pretended to head for school. She circled the block, waited for ten minutes, then came back home.

She told Noel about the dream. He didn't seem particularly impressed, but was obviously delighted at having some company.

He hung upside-down from a branch and played the violin for her while she sat in the straw. He played fast, intricate dance music, jigs and reels, while Tommy clapped along.

"That's what was being played last night," she said. "Just those sorts of tunes."

He tossed his head as if to say that this sort of stuff was almost too easy to be worth bothering with.

He dragged her into the front room and sat at the chess board.

"No," she said. "It's boring."

He frowned and rattled his claws on the board.

"I don't care," she said. "You can sulk all you want. I'm not interested."

109

He sulked for half an hour solid while Tommy doodled on the piano and tried to ignore him.

The doorbell rang. Tommy and Noel looked at each other with eyes round as soup bowls.

Tommy crept to the door and managed to slide one eye out into the hall. She could see a shadow – a shape through the leaded light panels in the front door. A tall, thin shape.

Noel tugged at her skirt. She patted him away.

The letterbox rattled. Tommy ducked out of sight.

She heard a voice. "Well?" it said. A honeyed voice. Pretorius, without a doubt.

"Hold your horses!" A voice like vinegar. Unity Hitch.

"Is there anyone there?"

"I see no one," said Hitch. "They've all gone out. Good. Very good."

Tommy glanced anxiously at Noel. He made bashing motions with his arm. She shook her head. Bashing them didn't seem like an appropriate idea. They were more likely to end up as bashees rather than bashers, Tommy couldn't help thinking.

The letterbox snapped shut. Tommy peeped round the door frame again. The shadow had gone.

Tommy crept to the front door and listened. There wasn't a sound. Not a whisper.

"What do you think?" she hissed at Noel.

He grabbed her arm and pointed to the back.

"Yes, I think you're right. We haven't got much time – what do we do?" She could phone the police, but Hitch and Pretorius could cause a lot of havoc before anyone arrived to save them. They could barricade themselves in an upper room and hope for the best. Dangerous. Dangerous to be cornered like that by two fiends who she knew were capable of murder. The only other alternative was to escape out of the front while they were gaining access through the back.

But even that would mean being out on the street and in full view of the deadly pair. Tommy had heard of people being dragged into cars and carried off in broad daylight. Not every day, but it did happen.

Then she had an idea. Her mother's car was out the front. The spare keys were in the hall cabinet. She and Noel could hide in the car. There was room for them to crouch down between the front and back seats, pull the blanket (kept for emergencies and picnics) over themselves, and lie low until her father arrived.

She found the keys. "Come on," she said. "I know where we'll be safe."

Noel scrambled up into her arms. There was a faint but very sharp tinkle of glass from the back of the house. From Noel's room. She opened the front door very quietly. She tiptoed out and peeped round the edge of the house, just in case one of the villains was standing guard.

The front garden was deserted. She crept down the path. The whole street was deserted. Not so much as a little old lady toddling off for her shopping. Tommy would have been very pleased to have seen a troop of hefty policemen marching up the road. Even a couple of relatively weedy policemen would have done. A police dog, even. With mange.

She unlocked the car and they slid inside.

Noel bounced into the driver's seat and held out a claw for the keys.

"Don't be ridiculous!" said Tommy. "Your feet don't reach the pedals and even if they did you couldn't see out of the front."

Noel clung grimly on to the wheel.

"We're hiding," said Tommy. "In the back. Come on, before we're seen."

She climbed over the back seat. She unfolded the blanket (emergencies and picnics). She stuck her head over the seat

111

back. Noel was perched on the edge of the seat, trying to reach the pedals with his hind claws.

"Noel, will you come over here before you're spotted?"

He shook his head and snapped his claws at her, demanding the keys.

"You're barmy," she said. "Get over here." She reached across and prised one set of claws off the steering wheel. She got an arm unlocked and set about the other. No sooner had that been prised free than the first claw latched on again.

"Noel, for heaven's sake! You can't drive this thing. You haven't got a licence." She managed to get both arms free and haul him backwards. He glared at her and clamped his back claws around the wheel.

"If you don't let go I'll bite your nose," she said.

He looked at her in disbelief.

"I will," she said. "Promise."

He allowed himself to be dragged unceremoniously over the back of the seat and down into the well between front and back seats. Tommy pulled the blanket over them.

Noel bundled himself into a sullen heap and glared at her.

"Can you really drive?" she said.

He nodded curtly. She blinked at him. It didn't seem very likely – it didn't seem possible – but he could do so many impossible things that Tommy couldn't be sure. One thing was certain though – if he did manage to get himself in a position to work the pedals and the steering wheel, there was no way in the world he'd be able to see out through the windscreen without a periscope.

They waited in hot, stuffy gloom for what seemed like a very long time.

"Dad'll be here soon," hissed Tommy, "And then we'll be safe."

Noel crawled over her and stuck his head out of the blanket to look through the side window.

"Get down," she whispered. Noel patted her head to let

112

her know it was all right. She pulled the blanket back and cautiously raised herself until her eyes were at window ledge level beside Noel. Nothing seemed to be happening.

She drew the blanket over their heads so that only their eyes were visible.

After another long wait the front door of their house opened. Hitch and Pretorius sneaked out and closed the door behind them. Their faces were angry and frustrated. Tommy hoped they hadn't caused too much chaos in the house in their futile search for Noel.

They walked down the path. Tommy dipped her head and pulled Noel down with her. She listened intently as the two sets of footsteps drew close.

"They've taken the creature," said Hitch. "Damn it! That fool Twigg."

"We've no time for recriminations," drawled Pretorius. "We must act and act fast. Twigg will be singing his heart out to the police if I know him."

"I told you he'd be the weak link."

"Yes, yes, my dear Hitch. And we've precious little time for 'I told you so's' either. The question is: do we make a final hell-for-leather attempt at getting the creature or do we slip away with our tails between our legs?"

"I won't be thwarted. We must have that creature. I *will* have that creature."

"Good. We're together on it, then. Good. So – we wait in the car, and when the first member of that dratted family turns up – probably that vile little girl – we get 'em. Find out where they've taken that creature ... "

"You've brought the gun?"

"Yes. I've brought the gun."

"Excellent. We get the creature, hand it over to your friends, take the money, and before anyone knows what's happening we're on an aeroplane to Brazil and a life of luxury and ease."

"Quite. My only regret being that I won't personally be able to supervise the experiments that are going to be performed on the creature."

Footsteps and voices receded. Tommy gave it a couple of minutes before she dared look out of the window again. Pretorius's little black maggot of a car was on the other side of the street. She could see the two of them sitting in it. They appeared to be eating sandwiches.

"They've got a gun!" she hissed to Noel. She peered between the front seats. The car clock showed a quarter to twelve. At any minute her father would be coming innocently along the street. And Hitch and Pretorius would be waiting. With a gun.

She looked anxiously at Noel.

"What do we do?"

But it didn't seem as if there was anything they *could* do, as the clock slowly ticked its way towards noon.

Chapter Fourteen

Tommy and Noel crouched hand in claw in the back of the car and waited.

After about five minutes Tommy heard voices. She sneaked a glance along the road. Her father and another man were walking towards them. She recognised the other man, although she had never seen more of him than his head and shoulders before. Mr Silk. Her father's driving instructor.

She dived down under the blanket. This called for very quick thinking. With Hitch and Pretorius on the other side of the road with a gun, it wasn't a good idea for her to leap up straight away. That much was obvious. If the two villains saw that her father wasn't alone they would probably do nothing. They would probably let him drive off, in the hope that they'd be able to catch some other member of the family on their own later on. Her, probably.

Yes. That was it. Tommy would keep herself hidden until her father had driven round the corner and then she would reveal herself and Noel. Her father would drive straight to the police station. Ten police cars would descend on Hitch and Pretorius and the whole affair would draw to a neat and satisfying conclusion.

At least, that was the plan.

She ducked down again as she heard her father and Mr Silk approaching.

"You've really got nothing to worry about, David. You're a perfectly competent driver. I wouldn't have put you in for the test if I didn't think you'd pass." Tommy heard the key in the lock. "Just remember to look in your mirror before every move you make."

The door opened and her father got into the driver's seat. He leaned across and flipped up the lock trigger on the passenger side and Mr Silk got in. Tommy and Noel drew themselves into tight, silent bundles under the blanket. Tommy began to wonder whether having long arms and legs was such a good idea. Fine for netball but very awkward for hiding in cars.

A hand came groping between the seats for the end of the seat belt. It missed Tommy's ear by half a centimetre. Noel picked up the seatbelt buckle and pushed it into the flailing fingers.

"Thank you," said Tommy's father, snapping the belt closed.

"Sorry?" said Mr Silk.

"Well," her father let out a long breath. "Off we go, then."

"Um … David … haven't you forgotten something?"

"Seat belt. Mirror. Wing mirrors."

"You haven't taken the steering wheel lock off."

"Ah."

Tommy's father unlocked the apparatus that kept the steering wheel secure. The engine purred.

"Ready for take-off," said Tommy's father. 'Chocks away!"

"Mirror," said Mr Silk.

"Yes. Right." Her father giggled. "Nearly forgot."

The car moved smoothly away from the kerb. Tommy was quite impressed. She'd been in the car with her father driving once before. Some months ago, admittedly. Most cars were driven by horsepower – under her father's guidance their car seemed to run on kangaroo-power. *Boing, boing, boing!* down the road, coughing and spluttering. Tommy had decided not to put her life in her father's hands again. Not if she could help it.

"Right turn," said Mr Silk, "At the junction."

"Mirror. Signal. Manoeuvre," said Tommy's father.

"It's not absolutely necessary to say it out loud every time," said Mr Silk. "It might hint to the examiner that you're not altogether sure of yourself."

The car slowed and moved to the centre of the road.

"Check your mirror," said Mr Silk.

"Oh, yes. I forgot."

"You're signalling left, David. We're turning right."

"Ooops!" Another giggle. Tommy held her face in her hands.

"Don't worry about it. Keep your eye on that car behind us. The Austin Cambridge." Mr Silk looked over his shoulder. "I haven't seen one of those for ages. I think they stopped making them in the fifties. Pretty little thing, isn't it? Like a little black beetle."

Tommy's heart jumped into her throat. A little black beetle. Pretorius and Hitch were following them. Tommy hadn't expected that. Best lie low for the time being. Hope they'd lose them in traffic. The idea of bullets whistling past their ears as they drove along didn't appeal to her in the least. Tommy's confusion wasn't helped when she noticed that Noel, on his back on the floor with his arms and legs wrapped around himself, seemed to have fallen asleep.

They drove on for a while.

"That car's still behind us," said Tommy's father.

"Yes. I know. Straight across at the traffic lights then follow the road round. The Driving Centre is down the second turning on the left. You're doing fine, David. There shouldn't be any problems this time ... "

"Mirror. Signal. Manoeuvre."

" ... so long as you stop saying that."

"Sorry."

They arrived at the Centre and Tommy's father switched the engine off.

"Okay," said Mr Silk. "You just sit tight for a minute and I'll go and check it out." Mr Silk got out of the car.

Tommy heard her father's fingers tapping nervously on the steering wheel. "Rum tum, tiddly-umpty tum," he said with leaden lightheartedness. "Mirror. Signal. Manoeuvre," he said. "Tiddly-ompty-pom." He whistled tunelessly and let out a long sigh.

Tommy thought it was probably time to reveal herself.

"Brrmmm, brrmmm," said her father.

Tommy slowly lifted her head over the back of the seat. Her father was sliding his hands round on the steering wheel. "Brmmm. Br-r-rmm. Meo-o-owww. Brrrr-ummm."

"Er ... Dad ...?"

He very nearly went through the roof of the car. She'd never heard him scream before.

Tommy smiled rigidly. "Hello," she said. "Surprise," she added.

He goggled at her, his mouth hanging open. "What the ... "

She heard the banging of a car door behind them. She snapped her head round. Pretorius and Hitch had parked and were out of their car and coming towards them.

"Quick!" yelled Tommy. "Get out of here! They've got a gun."

Her father sat staring at her in disbelief. "What ... the ... "

118

A greeny-brown streak of lightning whooshed over her father's shoulder and landed in his lap. Before her father had time to do anything, a claw had turned the key in the ignition and Noel had slid down between her father's knees and jammed his back claws on the pedals.

The car went off like a bullet..

"Aaarrrgh!" said her father as the road flew past. "Eowwowoweeearrrgh!"

Tommy was hurled backwards in a tangle of arms, legs and blanket. She unwrapped herself and looked out of the back window. Pretorius and Hitch were running back to their car.

She clung to the back of her father's seat. He was clutching the steering wheel in a blind panic.

The car raced along the road, gathering speed.

"Dad! Look out!"

He swung the steering wheel and they grazed past a parked lorry.

"Noel!" shouted Tommy. "Stop! You'll kill us."

They tore uphill and flew over the crest – all four wheels off the road.

"Tomm-ee-eearooop!" squawked her father. "Get 'im off! He-elp!"

"Emergency stop!" yelled Tommy.

Her father jammed his foot down hard on the brake. The car nose-dived into the tarmac and the back wheels bucked high in the air. The seat belt saved her father from going straight through the windscreen. Tommy hung around his neck as everything seemed to go over and over. All her innards seemed to swap places, like sweets being shaken up in a jar.

She hadn't even had a chance to recover before she heard a screech of brakes and a grinding, crashing, crunching noise behind them.

She gazed dizzily round. The back end of the Pretorius

car was sticking out of a huge hedge at the roadside. Leaves and bits of branch scattered the pavement. Dust was slowly settling.

Noel's face appeared between her father's knees, cross-eyed and woozy-looking.

A policeman was standing on the pavement, staring at them in disbelief. He walked slowly round to the off-side of the car and tapped on the glass. Tommy's father wound the window down.

"Mood gorning, ossifer," said her father. But the policeman wasn't looking at him. He was looking at the face that was beaming up at him from beneath the steering wheel.

Noel gave the policeman a victory salute from between Tommy's father's knees and slid slowly out of sight.

"I can explain," said Tommy. "Really. I can explain everything."

Pretorius, Hitch and Twigg went to prison for a long time. Tommy's father was allowed to take his driving test a couple of days later and passed with flying colours. Noel became a fully-accepted member of the family and they all lived together happily ever after.

That would have suited Tommy perfectly. Unfortunately, life didn't choose to tie itself into so neat a bow as that. Life decided to be a bit more complicated.

Alphonso Twigg was done for breaking and entering. He retracted everything he'd told Tommy and her mother about Great Aunt Tomasina's death, and actually accused them of assaulting him. Tommy and her mother were cautioned about taking the law into their own hands. Twigg got six months in an open prison and spent his time growing prize-winning marrows and telling anyone who would listen that none of it had been his fault at all, that he had always wanted to be a zoo keeper, and that life was treating him very harshly in the circumstances.

It proved impossible to pin anything on Unity Hitch. Sheer nastiness, as Tommy found out, was not sufficient reason under English law to lock a person away for the rest of their life. Tommy considered this to be a mistake. Sheer nastiness, said Tommy, ought to be the *perfect* reason for slinging someone in jail and throwing the key away.

Professor Pretorius was convicted of fraud. He spent his prison term writing his memoirs, entitled *It Shouldn't Happen to a Vivisectionist*. The book proved very popular, and on his release he went to live as a tax exile in Jersey.

Once Twigg took back everything he'd said in his inverted state in Noel's room, no evidence could be found to link the three villains to Great Aunt Tomasina's death and the Petheridge family didn't have the sort of money that they would have needed to bring a private prosecution.

A sort of peace settled on the Petheridge household.

"More toast, anyone?" asked Tommy's mother.

Noel nodded. He was sitting in his special high chair at the breakfast table. He had his broadsheet newspaper (delivered daily) folded in front of him and was rapidly filling in the cryptic crossword.

"Marmalade?" asked Tommy's mother.

Another preoccupied nod from Noel as he pushed his plate over.

"I wouldn't mind another slice of toast," said Tommy's father.

"You haven't got time," said Tommy's mother. "You'll be late for work."

He stood up and pulled his jacket on.

"Don't forget these," said Tommy, holding out his bicycle clips.

"Thank you," he said, taking them from her and securing the bottoms of his trouser legs. He coughed politely. "Um … might I have my newspaper?"

Noel entered the final crossword answer with a flourish and leaned back. He gestured airily to Tommy's father that he could take the paper. Tommy's father folded the newspaper under his arm.

"Right," he said. "I'll be off."

"Mmm," said Tommy's mother.

" 'Bye," said Tommy.

Noel waggled his claws.

Tommy's father looked perplexedly around the kitchen, sighed and wandered out.

"What are you two up to today, then?" asked Tommy's mother. It was the school holidays.

"Oh, this and that," said Tommy.

"This *and* that?" said her mother. "You'll be busy, then." She checked her lipstick in the mirror and picked up her briefcase. She looked at Noel. "Anything you want me to bring back?" Noel pushed a shopping list across the table to her. Their eating habits had become much more interesting since he had taken over the cooking. Life in general had become much more interesting now that Noel didn't spend all his time hanging in his glass room. Tommy's father wasn't really sure that he wanted life to be as interesting as it had become. Not that he was given the choice.

Tommy got up to see her mother off. Noel shambled across the table and clambered into her arms.

They stood on the doorstep, waving to her mother as she got into the car.

"Behave yourselves!" shouted her mother.

"Of course," said Tommy.

She closed the front door.

Noel wrapped his arm around Tommy's neck and let out a shrill, whooping whistle, just like he did every morning once they'd got the house to themselves.

"Well," Tommy said, with a big, happy grin on her face. "What shall we do, then?"

DASH

If you enjoyed this book, why not look out for other titles in the Dash series.

The Book of Lies by Toby Forward £2.99 ☐

In this fantastical tale of sorcery, illusions, treachery and revenge, James, Matthew and Wendy join forces with three royal Arabian children to do battle with an evil sorcerer who is threatening the King and his city.

Pony Patrol by Christine Pullein-Thompson £2.99 ☐

The Pony Patrol is a team of young riders who patrol the countryside on horseback – watching, investigating and protecting the peace of the land.

Other titles in the *Pony Patrol* series are:
Pony Patrol SOS £2.99 ☐
Pony Patrol Fights Back £2.99 ☐
Pony Patrol and the Mystery Horse £2.99 ☐

Ice Dancer by Mary Ross

An exciting series of books about one girl's dream to become a professional ice dancer.

Other titles in the *Ice Dancer* series are:
Robyn in a Spin £2.99 ☐
Robyn's Skating Challenge £2.99 ☐

All Simon & Schuster Young Books are available at your local bookshop or can be ordered direct from the publisher. Just tick the titles you want and fill in the form below. Prices and availability subject to change without notice.

Simon & Schuster Cash Sales Department, PO Box 11, Falmouth, Cornwall, TR10 9EN, England.

Please enclose a cheque or postal order to the value of the cover price and allow the following for postage and packing:
UK: 80p for the first book, and 20p for each additional book ordered up to a maximum charge of £12.00.
BFPO: 80p for the first book, and 20p for each additional book.
OVERSEAS & EIRE: £1.50 for the first book, £1.00 for the second book, and 30p for each subsequent book.

Name ....

Address ....

....

Postcode ....

Noel turned his curious, comical little face towards her. Tommy had never noticed before the way his wide mouth seemed almost to smile. A very particular smile. Not a happy-to-see-you type of smile, nor yet an I'm-having-a-nice-day kind of smile – more of an I-know-something-you-don't smile. But really, Tommy said to herself as she went back into the front room, *really* it's just the way his mouth *is*. Sloths don't really have knowing smiles on their faces any more than the expression on a cat's face is really smugness. It just looks that way.